THE EXTRAORDINARY ADVENTURES OF

ORDINARY BOY

BOOK THREE
THE GREAT POWERS OUTAGE

WILLIAM BONIFACE

ILLUSTRATIONS BY STEPHEN GILPIN

HarperCollins*Publishers*

Library of Congress Cataloging-in-Publication Data
Boniface, William.
    The great powers outage / William Boniface ; illustrations by Stephen Gilpin.
— 1st ed.
        p.   cm. — (The extraordinary adventures of Ordinary Boy ; bk. 3)
    ISBN 978-0-06-077470-7 (trade bdg.)
    [1. Heroes—Fiction.] I. Gilpin, Stephen, ill. II. Title.
PZ7.B6416Gr 2008   2007049579
[Fic]—dc22   CIP
                                                                                AC

Typography by R.Hult
2 3 4 5 6 7 8 9 10

First Edition

For my sister Carla, who was never allowed to touch my comic books—and still isn't.

Pinprick Manor

Needlepoint Hill

Carlsbark Caverns

CARBUNKLE MOUNTAINS

SUBURBIA

Westing Ho
Retirement

Telomere Park entrance

Crater Hill

Ordinary Boy's House

Watso
Element

SUBURBIA

Windbag's Junkyard

D
D

Dr. Telomere's Potato Chip Factory

Corpsicle Coolant Corp.

irrigation pools

INDUSTRIAL

I.I.

potato fields

SUPEROPOLIS
(AND ITS ENVIRONS)

ORNERY

OCEAN

SUPEROPOLIS HARBOR

lighthouse

Hero's Cape

SS *Befuddlement* wreck

City Hall

TOITY ROW

HOITY-

warehouse district

Mt. Reliable

LAVA PARK

museum

MEGAMANLY BEACH

BOARDWALK amusement park

VERTIGO BUILDING

DOWNTOWN

opera

TREMOR PARK

retail area

avalcade f Candy

retail area

ropolis Zoo

INDESTRUCTO INDUSTRIES

RESIDENTIAL

PROLOGUE

Great Ball o' Fire

The meteor was hurtling toward me and there was nothing I could do to stop it. I tried launching my body into the air, willing myself to fly, but with no luck. The fireball got closer and closer, and just as it was about to hit I raised my arm to ward it off, knowing it was futile.

And then I woke up, safe in bed, drenched in a cold sweat. It took me a moment to realize I had been dreaming. It was the cool air of the October night drifting across my skin, raising a field of goose bumps, that finally convinced me there wasn't a flaming meteor coming.

But there *had* been, less than two days earlier. In fact all Superopolis had been facing complete destruction at the hands of Professor Brain-Drain.

The evil genius had succeeded in his plan to transport the entire city sixty-five million years into the past to the very moment when the site that would become Superopolis had been formed by the impact of an enormous meteor. His plan had been for the city to be destroyed by the same event that created it.

The neat symmetry of his plot hadn't distracted me from the realization that it was up to me to stop him. With the help of a villain named Cyclotron, and one of Professor Brain-Drain's own gadgets, I had used a little ingenuity of my own to return Superopolis to the present just in the nick of time. In the end, Cyclotron turned out not to be a villain after all, and Professor Brain-Drain was marooned one hundred and thirty million years in the past.

That's the short version. Along the way, in the guise of the legendary hero Meteor Boy, I also spent a couple of days twenty-five years in the past battling evil. Wait a minute—let me clarify that. I wasn't disguised as Meteor Boy—I *was* Meteor Boy, one of the most powerful young heroes in the history of Superopolis. The irony of all this is that I'm actually the *least* powerful hero in the history of Superopolis. They don't call me Ordinary Boy for nothing.

You see, Superopolis is a city of heroes—and

villains—and every one of them has a superpower. Except me. But, thanks to a trip through time courtesy of Professor Brain-Drain's Time Tipler and a mysterious jet pack that allowed me to fly at tremendous speeds, I had the thrill of spending two days battling crime as Meteor Boy—and I had loved it!

During my adventure in the past I made the acquaintance of the League of Goodness, Superopolis's first and greatest team of heroes. The team's leader, Lord Pincushion, provided me hospitality and an opportunity to fight alongside him and the rest of the league. I'm not so sure I did him much of a favor in return. I introduced him to the Amazing Indestructo.

The thing you need to know about AI (that's what everyone calls him for short) is that up until a couple of weeks ago, he was my absolute favorite hero. He's totally indestructible, which gives him a pretty good advantage over any villain, and he's turned the hero business into a hugely profitable enterprise. Between his TV show, toy lines, packaged food business, and dozens of other endeavors, AI has become incredibly wealthy. The problem is all those things come ahead of actually battling crime. He's really kind of a creep, to tell the truth. It took me a while to realize it, and most of the population still hasn't figured it out.

The only part of my trip to the past that still makes me a little queasy is the fact that I was the one who suggested AI join forces with the League of Goodness. It had been for the best of reasons. The league was bankrupt from the expense of fighting crime, and the Amazing Indestructo needed a well-known name to launch his own career. The league provided the name, and AI soon provided the money.

Sadly, it didn't take long for AI to drive the founding members out of the league and replace them with the most incompetent array of nitwits you could imagine. He changed their name to the League of *Ultimate* Goodness, and set himself up to be the team's most impressive member.

My own father had tried to join the LUG a bunch of times. He never realized what a compliment it was that they wouldn't have him. His name is Thermo. He has the ability to generate enormous levels of heat in his hands. For most of my life he had a job at Dr. Telomere's Potato Chip Factory heating their massive fryers. But prior to that he had been part of a superhero team called the New Crusaders.

That's where he met my mom, Snowflake. She can freeze anything solid just by looking at it. She has a great job at the Corpsicle Coolant Corporation, although I've never really known what she does there. Here's the entry for CCC in the *Li'l Hero's Handbook*. The handbook has sections on all the people, places, and even some of the things in Superopolis. I carry it with me constantly!

CORPSICLE COOLANT CORPORATION

From its earliest success when it applied for—and received—a patent on winter, CCC has dominated the market for subzero products. Their Chilled Gills line of frozen fish and their Frigi-Fries line of frozen potato products have all been hits. Equally successful is their Vegicles line of frozen vegetables, despite the notable failure of their advertising campaign to convince kids that their vegetables were made by elves who lived in a magic igloo.

Because of the money my mom makes, Dad was able to quit his job at Dr. Telomere's and return to crime fighting. He joined some of his former teammates and they're calling themselves the New New Crusaders . . . and, no, that's not a misprint.

Of course, there's one thing I miss about his old job, and that's the unlimited supply of free potato chips. Boy, do we eat a lot of them! So does everyone in Superopolis. In fact, the only business more successful than the Amazing Indestructo's is Dr. Telomere's chip factory.

I'm sure it drives AI crazy, but there's nothing he can do about it. Nothing beats the salty, fried goodness of a bag of Dr. Telomere's potato chips.

Mmmm . . . potato chips. With that pleasant thought I felt my eyes drifting shut once again. But only a moment later I was reawakened by a familiar voice.

"Thank you for saving me, O Boy."

I opened my eyes and found myself atop Crater Hill in the center of Telomere Park. It was still the middle of the night. I was dressed in my Meteor Boy costume, and standing in front of me was the cartoon figure of Dr. Telomere, a potato chip wearing a derby hat, pince-nez glasses, and a bow tie. The thought that I was dreaming again never even occurred to me as I talked with the advertising spokescharacter of Dr. Telomere's Potato Chip Company.

"You're welcome," I answered, as if talking to a potato chip was a routine situation. "But how could I have saved you if you're not real?"

"Aren't I?" he replied with concern as his gloved hands patted at his potato chip body. "Oh dear. Then are any of us real?"

"I'm real!" I insisted. "I think."

"Only because of *that*, boy!" The potato chip pointed to the night sky. "Only because of *that*."

I looked up and there it was again—a huge flaming meteor heading right for me. I turned back to the potato chip, but he was gone—replaced by the sinister, cackling presence of Professor Brain-Drain. I jolted awake—once more back in my bed. But the image of the fireball stayed with me. I may have escaped it, but it *had* hit the piece of land where Superopolis now sits. The effects of a collision of that magnitude must have been enormous. Now wide awake, I couldn't help but wonder if an event like that might still be affecting things even all these millions of years later.

CHAPTER ONE

Tossed Salad

I couldn't believe what I was seeing. A group of vegetables had just robbed the Mighty Mart! I know that sounds ridiculous, but it was true. Even now, an enormous stalk of celery was crossing the parking lot heading right for me. Okay, so maybe it wasn't *really* a giant piece of celery (not that such a thing was impossible in Superopolis), but it *was* a guy dressed like one. And he was trying to get away with a large bag of Maximizer Brand Booster Bars.

But just as he tried to escape with his loot, a powerful blast of air knocked him to the ground, courtesy of the hero Windbag. As the startled vegetable struggled to get back on his feet, a large ear of corn pushing a shopping cart filled with Maximizer Brand Superdoodlers tripped and fell on top of him.

"You're stepping on my leaves, Colonel Corncob," yelled the celery. "Watch where you're going!"

I almost started clapping as my father, the mighty Thermo, strode up to the crumpled vegetables and lifted Colonel Corncob off the flustered stalk of celery.

"The only place you'll be going, Celery Stalker, is prison!"

"Tarnation!" hollered Colonel Corncob as he got a taste of my dad's power. "I'm feelin' hotter than a peck of pipin' peppers!"

A second later, some of the Colonel's kernels exploded in my father's grasp. Amid the confusion, the Celery Stalker made his escape. He didn't get far before another hero grabbed him and hoisted him effortlessly into the air.

"The Levitator!" I cheered, as my dad's teammate used his power to levitate the human-size celery stalk. Wrapping his hands around the villain's ankles, he began swinging him around in a circle.

"Batter up!" He laughed as he spun the Celery Stalker faster and faster.

"And here's the pitch!" someone added from across the parking lot.

There, another member of my dad's team, the Big Bouncer, was rolling toward a horrified-looking onion. Actually, only his head looked like an onion—

NAME: Levitator, The. **POWER:** Can make anything weightless just by touching it. **LIMITATIONS:** Except himself. **CAREER:** Following the disbanding of the New Crusaders, the Levitator became a dietitian whose happy clients always held his hand when weighing in. **CLASSIFICATION:** An all-around lighthearted guy.

or more precisely, a shallot. Regardless, as the Big Bouncer smashed into him, he went flying toward the swinging stalk of celery. The Levitator smacked the onion-headed guy with the Celery Stalker, and he went flying across the parking lot, leaving a shower of Maximizer Brand Fudge Brawnies, raining down on the startled onlookers.

With everyone's attention focused on the shower of snack cakes, an irritated-looking chickpea came running up to my father.

"What da heck are youse guys doin'?!" he sputtered in frustration. "Da script says dat we's s'posed to be roughin' youse guys up at foist."

"Oh, sorry, Garbanzo," my dad said, raising his hands defensively as he backed away from Colonel Corncob, who was now missing several kernels from his body.

"Dat's da *Great* Garbanzo to youse," the cigar-chomping chickpea responded with disgust as he motioned forward another member of his "gang." "Now let da Broccoli Robber here rough youse up some."

The Broccoli Robber was definitely a guy in a costume. His fists were sheathed in big, poofy gloves that looked like broccoli florets. He nervously approached my dad and began punching him feebly. My father almost looked sorry for the guy.

"You could at least *act* like I'm hurting you," the

Broccoli Robber whined between breaths.

"Oh, sure," Dad replied. "Sorry about that."

"I'm powerless . . . against . . . broccoli," he said in what was supposed to be a weakened voice. He then fell to the ground beneath the Broccoli Robber's blows.

"Man, your dad is a lousy actor."

I turned to my best friend, Stench, who was standing beside me.

"Yeah, I know," I admitted. "Your dad is actually pretty good though."

We both looked over to where Stench's dad, Windbag, was on his knees in front of the guy with the onion head. He was bawling his eyes out.

"No, he's pretty bad, too," Stench said. "That guy's head actually *is* an onion and he's making my dad's eyes water."

Looking around I realized that none of the members of my dad's team, the New New Crusaders, were very good actors. The Levitator was practically throwing himself at the feet of the Celery Stalker, who could barely maneuver in his unwieldy costume. Not far from them Colonel Corncob was trying to lasso the Big Bouncer, who was standing completely still to make the task easier.

"Now youse guys see da effects dat vegetables can

have on youse." The Great Garbanzo laughed as he got everyone back on script. "Youse heroes is too weak to even fight back!"

Okay, so maybe this wasn't the most honest representation of the "dangers" of vegetables. But, then again, no one here was trying to sell vegetables.

"Must . . . increase . . . strength," my dad said robotically as he reached for one of the scattered packages of Maximizer Brand MaxiMuffins.

Ripping off the wrapper, my dad gave a performance he didn't need to fake as he shoved the muffins into his mouth. A moment later he slowly got to his feet and delivered another wooden line.

"I feel my energy returning," he said. "Listen up, New New Crusaders. These Maximizer Brand snack cakes can give us back the strength these vile vegetables have sapped from us."

The Broccoli Robber backed away nervously.

"And the first thing coming off the menu"—Thermo smacked a fist into his hand—"is broccoli."

Dad lunged for the frightened guy in the broccoli costume as the rest of his teammates helped themselves to the scattered snack cakes. The Levitator made light work of the Celery Stalker, grabbing him with both hands and launching him into the air. The piercing scream of the celery ended the moment he landed atop the fleeing Broccoli Robber.

"Ah say, sir, you are no gentleman," Colonel Corncob sputtered as the Big Bouncer hurtled toward him. If he thought words could stop the rubbery hero, he was mistaken. BB smacked into him and sent the ear of corn flying—minus another half dozen kernels from his body.

The guy with the onion head was making a serious attempt to use his power, but Windbag had learned his lesson and stood safely out of range.

"Cry. Cry! CRY!" the shallot shrieked hysterically.

"Watch this!" Stench elbowed me as his dad took an enormous breath.

On cue, Windbag exhaled with such incredible force that the onion-headed guy was blown head over heels into the accumulating pile of vegetables.

"Now that's what I call onion breath,"

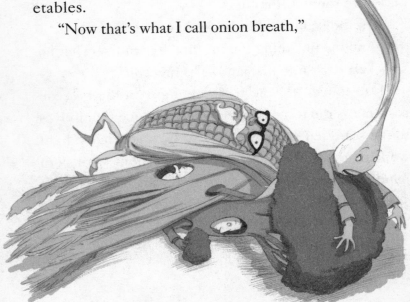

my father said stiffly, following the script. "There's only one item this tasteless salad is lacking."

With that, each of the four New New Crusaders grabbed a different one of the Great Garbanzo's limbs. When they had a firm hold, they began swinging him back and forth.

"Is dis da end of da Great Garbanzo?" the giant chickpea asked dramatically at the height of one of the swings.

"One . . . two . . . three," the New New Crusaders chanted in unison before releasing the Great Garbanzo into the air.

"Brace my fall, boys," I heard him say to his horrified team members as he flew toward them. They tried to scatter, but he got there too fast and crushed them beneath him.

With the medley of "criminal" vegetables practically pureed, my father turned to the crowd that had assembled behind us.

"Vegetables just can't compare to the power of Maximizer Brand snack cakes," he said dramatically.

Stench and I immediately started clapping but quickly realized we were the only ones doing so. We turned around in surprise. There had been at least two hundred people here in the parking lot of the Mighty Mart when the performance began, but now there was no one to be seen. The crowd had vanished.

"Where is everyone?" my dad asked with alarm. "They're missing the debut of the New New Crusaders as the official spokesteam for Maximizer snack cakes."

"Maximizer *Brand* snack cakes," corrected an irritated Great Garbanzo as he got off his groaning comrades. "How many times does I needs to remind youse dat we always has to say "brand"? It prevents us from infringin' on da manufacturer of shoe lifts wit da same name."

"Look." Stench pointed. "The crowd has moved to the far side of the parking lot."

Sure enough, something else *had* caught the eye of the crowd—something even more exciting than a group of villainous vegetables. Even from where we were standing there was no mistaking who it was—Superopolis's greatest (self-proclaimed) superhero—the Amazing Indestructo.

CHAPTER TWO

New and Improved?

The look of annoyance in my father's eyes couldn't have been plainer. His team's big debut had been spoiled by the Amazing Indestructo. The Great Garbanzo was even more peeved.

"Let me at dat so-and-so," he cursed. "If he's here to push his own line a snack cakes at da expense a mine, I'll break botha his legs and den his arms just ta make soiten he gets da message."

"But, boss," said the guy in the broccoli suit, "he's indestructible."

"I'll shows youse indestructible," he said as he barged past the broccoli, knocking him to the ground.

My dad and his teammates hesitated for a moment but then followed the fuming legume. After all, he was their new boss. The Great Garbanzo was the owner of

NAME: Great Garbanzo, The. **POWER:** High in protein. **LIMITATIONS:** Low in flavor. **CAREER:** When his line of hummus breakfast products failed miserably, the dispirited Garbanzo abandoned all his strongly held beliefs on healthy eating and started the Maximizer Brand Snack Cake Company. It was an immediate success. **CLASSIFICATION:** A sugary triumph has only led to a sour disposition.

the Maximizer Brand Snack Cake Company. Stench and I went along, too.

As we walked across the parking lot the throng continued to grow. AI's ability to draw a crowd went far beyond that of the New New Crusaders', and he stood silently, basking in the admiration, atop a makeshift stage that had been built for this appearance. Lined up behind him were six of the ten members of the League of Ultimate Goodness: the Crimson Creampuff; Featherweight; Moleman; the Human Compass; Cap'n Blowhole; and my personal favorite, Whistlin' Dixie.

As soon as Dixie started whistling the Amazing Indestructo theme song—perfectly in tune, of course—the crowd quieted to a low murmur. AI waited a moment or two longer and then began to speak.

"I know that you, the good citizens of Superopolis, expect nothing but the finest when it comes to products bearing the Amazing Indestructo name," he began in a serious tone. "I take great pride in the restraint I've shown throughout my career in not releasing just any old merchandise for the sake of a quick buck."

A mocking snort erupted from deep inside me. People nearby turned and glared, but my dad gave me an approving pat on the shoulder.

"Which is why," AI continued, oblivious to my editorial outburst, "I am proud to announce that, after more than a decade in development, Indestructo

Industries has produced a potato chip worthy of the Amazing Indestructo name!"

I think he was expecting a massive roar of approval from the crowd, but all he got was a stunned silence. He plowed ahead anyway.

"Superopolis, I'm proud to present to you the Amazing Indestructo's Amazing Pseudo-Chips!"

We all watched in astonishment as four enormous cylinders rose from each corner of the stage. They were designed to look like canisters of AI's Amazing Pseudo-Chips, and each bore the tagline "Every Chip as Perfect as Him!" No one in the crowd had ever seen anything like this before—with the exception of me.

Less than a week earlier, I had not only gotten a sneak peek at these odd-

looking potato chips that stacked in a can, I even used the can as a component in the fully functional time machine I created as a science fair project. I should have known it was only a matter of time before the Amazing Indestructo attempted to launch them as a new product line. But even he faced an enormous hurdle in making them a success.

"Potato chips?" I heard someone mutter. "Why would we buy any chips other than Dr. Telomere's?"

Similar comments were filtering through the crowd when the tops of the four enormous canisters exploded and potato chips—make that *Pseudo*-Chips—began raining down on the startled spectators. People frantically tried catching the crispy projectiles, and those who were successful popped them into their mouths. Meanwhile, the members of the League of Ultimate Goodness had moved to the forefront to perform

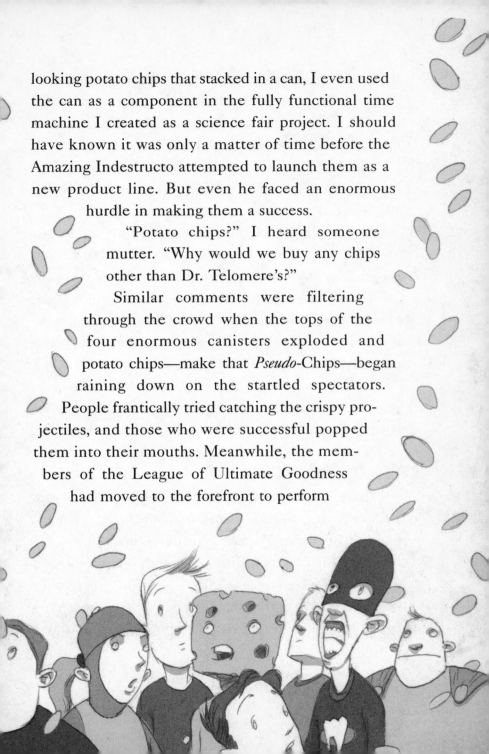

their individual parts in this crass, commercial enterprise.

"There's only one direction to follow for true potato chip–like flavor, and that's to AI's Amazing Pseudo-Chips," proclaimed the Human Compass.

"They're plum gar-un-teed to leave ya whistlin' fer more," Whistlin' Dixie said, tipping her rhinestone-studded cowgirl hat.

Featherweight stepped forward and raised a finger as if he were about to speak, but then a stiff wind caught him and whipped him into the air.

"They're as light and crispy as . . . ," I think I heard him say before the breeze whisked him—and whatever his analogy was going to be—out of earshot. His teammates carried on without missing a beat.

"Aaargh, mateys!" agreed Cap'n Blowhole as a plume of water shot out of the top of his head. "Discovering Pseudo-Chips is like finding buried treasure . . . except you'll find them aboveground . . . and they're not really made out of gold."

"Regular, boring chips contain only potatoes, oil, and salt," the Crimson Creampuff informed the audience. "But the Amazing Indestructo's Amazing Pseudo-Chips contain dozens of ingredients, most of which are unpronounceable!"

"They have an earthy flavor . . . like something that's just been dug from the ground," announced

Moleman, as everyone on the stage, including AI, turned and glared at him. "I meant that as a compliment," he added meekly.

But the crowd was having none of it. We had spent a lifetime eating Dr. Telomere's potato chips, and anything else seemed like heresy. I couldn't help but smile at the thought that I was witnessing a monumental financial defeat for the Amazing Indestructo. He had finally pushed his luck one chip too far.

He realized it, too. In a panic, he turned to another figure on the stage who I hadn't noticed until now. It was an older man dressed all in red, and AI ushered him up to the microphone.

"And here to speak about yet another of the tremendous benefits of AI's Pseudo-Chips is our official spokesman, Comrade Crunch."

There was something about the intensity of this silver-haired old man that made the crowd go silent. He strode purposefully to the microphone, and his gaze washed over us. For a moment it felt like his eyes had focused on me, and me alone. Instinctively I knew that every person standing here had experienced the same sensation. Then he began to speak.

"Comrades," he began in an aged yet powerful voice. "A new day is upon us. For decades we have been told what we like and what we don't like when it comes to salty, fried snacks. A force beyond our control has guided us down one particular path, telling us that there is only one choice when it comes to something as important as potato chips."

The crowd was hanging on every word. In fact, so was I. His statements sure *felt* compelling, but what was he really saying? It was difficult, but I forced myself to focus on Comrade Crunch's message rather than on how it was making me feel.

"But now, at long, long last, we have a choice. Open your eyes! That single path has finally reached a fork in the road. Will you continue down the path to the right? A path

that has been laid out for you as if you had no mind of your own? Or will you take the path to the left? This is a new path, an exciting path! A path you choose for *yourself*. Are you ready to try a new kind of potato chip?"

"YES!" the audience erupted in unison.

"Are you ready to take a new path?" Comrade Crunch shouted even louder.

"YES!" the crowd exploded in response, including my dad and Stench. What was happening here? That speech had made no sense!

"Then express your collective will," the old man in red built to a crescendo. "And take that path to the left. Amazing Indestructo Pseudo-Chips were made just . . . for . . . YOU!"

As if they had one mind, the crowd expressed their preference by turning en masse to the left and toward the grocery store. The Mighty Mart was about to sell a whole lot of potato chips, but they weren't going to be Dr. Telomere's.

CHAPTER THREE

A New Day Dawns

I came downstairs the next morning to find my mom and dad quarreling. It didn't take a genius to know what the argument was over. It had begun the moment Dad and I returned home from the Mighty Mart the day before.

"What got into your head?" Mom asked yet again as she gestured at the sixty or so canisters of Amazing Indestructo Pseudo-Chips that were stacked on every counter in the kitchen.

Normally, when Mom gets this mad, Dad immediately apologizes—even if he doesn't really think he's done anything wrong. That strategy has kept them together for years. But in the case of the Pseudo-Chips, he just wasn't budging.

"These chips are the future," he insisted. "We've

been forced to eat one brand our entire lives, and now we finally have a choice."

"But we've always loved Dr. Telomere's chips," my mom pointed out. "You used to work there! Why do you suddenly think there's something wrong with them?"

"It's not them," my father insisted, "but rather the opportunity to take a new path; to try something different."

He was parroting exactly what Comrade Crunch had said.

"They don't even taste good," my mom said in frustration as she sampled one of the chips.

I grabbed one of our remaining bags of Dr. Telomere's potato chips and headed for the TV room. I turned on the set and plopped onto the couch. The latest episode of *The Amazing Adventures of the Amazing Indestructo (and the League of Ultimate Goodness)* was on, but I had no intention of watching it. I no longer had any respect for AI and refused to support him in any way.

I flipped around and finally stopped on a channel running a Sunday morning news show. The banner across the bottom of the screen identified the program as *The Great Superopolis Mayoral Debate*. The announcer was in the process of explaining the setup.

". . . and with the election now only sixteen days

away, we're proud to be hosting the first in a series of debates. On your right is the incumbent candidate, Mayor Whitewash."

The camera turned to a podium where the mayor stood. He was smiling in his usual forced-casual sort of way and waving to the TV audience.

"And since the mayor is once again running unopposed," the announcer continued, "we'll represent his opponent in this debate with the prize-winning pumpkin from the recent Carbunkle County fair. We've even carved a face on it to increase the level of tension between the two debaters."

This was quite possibly the stupidest thing that I'd ever seen on TV, and that was saying a lot. I mean, there was no mystery why Mayor Whitewash was unopposed. Take a look at his entry in the *Li'l Hero's Handbook* and you'll see why.

A general sense of agreement was usually all it took for people to cast their votes for Mayor Whitewash. Of course, to actually force people to go out and vote for him would require a much stronger power—like the one I witnessed from Comrade Crunch yesterday. If the mayor had had *that* kind of ability, there would have been no need to stage a debate between him and a carved pumpkin.

"To get things started," the announcer continued,

LI'L HERO'S HANDBOOK
★ PEOPLE ★

NAME: Mayor Whitewash. **POWER:** The ability to make people agree with him. **LIMITATIONS:** Just because they agree with him doesn't mean they'll get off their butts and go vote for him. **CAREER:** Despite a formidable handicap in his first election, Whitewash has gone on to twelve consecutive terms as mayor. **CLASSIFICATION:** Utterly incompetent, yet highly electable.

"I'm pleased to welcome our guest moderator and member of the League of Ultimate Goodness—Mannequin!"

There was a weak smattering of applause from the tiny studio audience as Superopolis's greatest supermodel made her appearance. She was clearly perturbed by the mediocre response.

"Zank you for zat vonderful reception," she said, her voice dripping with sarcasm.

She stalked over to the table facing the two podiums and took her seat with all the flair one would expect from a fashion model with zero journalistic credibility.

"Zee first question is to you Mayor Vhitevash," Mannequin began. "As vith makeup, a good foundation is ezzential for good government. Vhat have you done vhile mayor to create such a foundation from vhich beauty can flourish?"

The camera switched to Mayor Whitewash, whose expression showed he clearly had no clue what Mannequin was asking. But like any good politician, that didn't stop him from answering.

"Why of course, madam moderator," he said with a courteous bow. "But first, I must tell you how beguiling you look this morning."

Despite the mayor's ability to make people agree with him, his power wasn't necessary in this case. Mannequin had no doubt that she was beguiling.

"In answer to your question," he continued. "Beauty is in the eye of the beholder, and I'm certainly beholding it now."

Mannequin blushed, completely ignoring the fact that he hadn't answered her question at all. She turned next to the carved pumpkin.

"Ze question I have for you, Mr. Pumpkinhead, is more zerious," she said in her *zerious* tone of voice. "How can von be avare of zee importance of beauty if von . . . vell, how does von say it? . . . if von looks . . . like a pumpkin, and not a very attractive von at that."

The camera turned to the pumpkin, which, not surprisingly, said nothing at all—-although it did appear to have a hurt expression carved on it. The camera remained fixed on it for the full two-minute response time. As this silent mockery of broadcast journalism continued, my parents entered the room.

"Why is there a pumpkin on the screen?" my father asked.

"I think it's running for mayor," I responded. "What's up?"

"I'd like to know what you think of these

chips, OB," my mom said. "I don't know why your father is obsessed with them. Maybe if he hears your opinion he'll realize he's been brainwashed."

"I don't get them, either," I agreed, "but I told him that as he was clearing them off the shelves at the Mighty Mart along with the rest of the mob. He wouldn't listen to me."

Just then the pumpkin's two minutes ended, and the announcer used the opportunity to cut away to a commercial. I sat up with alarm when the face of Comrade Crunch appeared on the screen.

"Perfection is at your fingertips, Superopolis," he began. "Who wants to deal with the sloppiness of potato chips that all look different from each other? Chips like that are drains on our society, competing with one another for attention instead of focusing on the common good. But I'm pleased to announce this potato chip problem has finally been fixed. Just like the hero himself, every Amazing Indestructo Pseudo-Chip is a paragon of preformed perfection. No greasy textures. No wasted packaging. NO INDIVIDU-ALITY! Each chip works in unison with every other for the common, crispy goodness of all! What's more, they'll make you smarter and better looking!" As he concluded, his voice rose to a crescendo. "This is Comrade Crunch telling everyone to go forth and buy the Amazing Indestructo's Amazing Pseudo-Chips in place of any other potato chip brand!"

For a moment I felt dazed. Then I had an overwhelming desire to shove aside my bag of Dr. Telomere's chips. But I shook myself free of that thought.

"This guy is dangerous," I said as I turned to look at my parents. The expressions on their faces were as blank as could be.

"I see your point, dear," my mother responded without even looking at Dad. "We do need to buy more of these chips. They'll even make us more attractive."

"And smarter," my father added dully.

Before I could get a grip on what had just happened, my parents bolted from the room and then from the house. Despite the sixty cans of potato chips already sitting in our kitchen, they were heading out to buy more! What had gotten into them? With worry welling up from the pit of my stomach, I turned back to the TV just as the grinning face of Comrade Crunch vanished from the screen.

CHAPTER FOUR

The Curious Case of Comrade Crunch

Something was horribly wrong. Crazy, illogical behavior from my father wasn't anything unusual. But from my mother, it was a different story. She almost always kept her cool, as one would expect from a hero named Snowflake. And she never willingly went along with Dad's nutty ideas. But that's exactly what had happened today.

I glanced at the clock. It was just about time for the regular weekly emergency meeting of the Junior Leaguers. There was something fishy about Comrade Crunch and I was going to need the help of my friends to figure out what it was.

When I arrived at our headquarters—the tree house in Stench's backyard—my friends were already gathered.

Surrounding them were dozens of canisters of Amazing Indestructo Pseudo-Chips.

"I know we aren't supposed to be doing anything to support AI," Plasma Girl said with a guilty shrug as she misinterpreted the look of concern on my face, "but we couldn't help ourselves."

"I think we should make Comrade Crunch our new favorite hero," Halogen Boy suggested. "You know . . . instead of AI."

"These chips are fantastic," Tadpole agreed. "How do you suppose AI managed to outdo Dr. Telomere's?"

That's what I wanted to know. These chips weren't "fantastic." They didn't taste bad, exactly, but they certainly didn't taste like real potato chips. And even if they had, it didn't explain this sudden mania that had gripped everyone.

"What made you guys go out and buy all these chips?" I asked.

"It was Comrade Crunch," Halogen Boy explained as his natural glow began to brighten. "He was on TV all morning talking about them."

"It's true." Stench nodded. "He was talking about how Pseudo-Chips can enhance our powers."

"What made you believe that?" I pressed. "Was it just because he said it?"

"It must be true," Hal said quietly. "It was on TV."

"I thought we had figured out that most of what's

on TV isn't true by the time we were ten," I sputtered.

"Comrade Crunch wouldn't lie," Tadpole asserted as if he were defending his own grandfather.

"Guys! Comrade Crunch is the one who is behind all this!" I finally blurted out my suspicion. "And I think it's time we learned a little bit more about him."

I pulled out my copy of the *Li'l Hero's Handbook* and flipped it open to the letter C. *The Codpiece, Collapso, the Collector, the Comforter . . . ! Concreto!* He wasn't there. For the first time ever, I had found someone who did not have an entry in the *Li'l Hero's Handbook*! How could that be? Unless it wasn't his real name. But then who was Comrade Crunch?

Just then pandemonium erupted all around us, and it looked like there were people everywhere! Our heads were spinning as we tried to focus on them. Then, just as quickly, they all came together in the form of a single person standing in front of us—a very *fast* person. One that none of us was happy to see.

"It's my brother's friend Zitty," Stench said, completely enraged. "Get out of our headquarters, you creep!"

"The name is *Zippy*," the teenage delinquent said as the acne on his face merged into a bright red flush of anger. "And don't forget it, Fart Face."

The speedy jerk whipped back into motion and

attacked Stench from all sides at once. He was too fast
for Stench to get hold of, and Zippy had soon maneuvered him to the entrance of our tree house. There
Stench had no choice but to climb down to escape the
older boy's pummeling blows. I clenched my own fists
in frustration. If I had still possessed my Meteor Boy
jet pack, Zippy would have been no match for me. But
my brief stint having a power was behind me.

The four of us were left alone in our headquarters,
but not for long. A second later Stench's brother, Fuzz
Boy, popped his head through the same entry that
Stench had just been driven out of.

"What have we here?" he said as he lunged for Halogen Boy. He soon had his hands all over Hal's face and body, and blond hair began to sprout everywhere.

"Stop it, you creep," Plasma Girl screeched, but Fuzz Boy just reached out and covered her mouth with his hand. She instantly reduced herself to a pool of goo and escaped.

Fuzz Boy looked at his empty hand in surprise. A moment later that expression turned to shock as Tadpole's tongue snaked around his torso, trapping his arms against his body. The clever move backfired, though, when Fuzz Boy got an arm loose and grabbed Tadpole's tongue. As hair began sprouting, Tadpole loosened his tongue in panic and Fuzz Boy got his other arm free, too. Then, to Tadpole's complete horror, Fuzz Boy began working his way hand over hand up the length of the tongue.

"Let's get out of here, guys," I hollered in desperation. I guided a dazed Halogen Boy through the door in the floor and followed right after him. Tadpole finally freed his tongue from Fuzz Boy's grasp and came tumbling after us, while Plasma Girl oozed her way through a crack in the floor.

Outside, amid the piles of scrap in his dad's junkyard, Stench was still warding off blows as Zippy darted around him.

"Stench," I yelled. "Retreat!"

He heard me and reluctantly ran after us. By the time we reached the street, Zippy had stopped pursuing. He'd probably gone back to plunder our tree house with Fuzz Boy.

"We gotta go back and take care of those creeps!" Stench fumed.

"No way," Plasma Girl said in disgust as she rematerialized. She only then realized that she had a thick beard where Fuzz Boy had covered her mouth with his hand. "Look what that creep did to me! He even got my lips!"

"Wht abt me?" Tadpole mumbled as best he could. He was holding about six feet of furry tongue that he refused to draw back into his mouth.

"I look like a giant fuzz ball," was all Hal would say.

"We can't go back without a plan," I insisted. "And we can't make a plan until the effects of this attack have worn off. What use would Hal or Tadpole be in their current condition? For now let's just get as far away as possible."

Considering how strange some people in Superopolis look, we didn't get too many stares as Stench and I accompanied our hair-covered trio of friends toward downtown and Lava Park. That seemed as good a place as any to hang out while we waited for them to return to normal.

When we reached the park, we headed for the entrance near the Inkblot's newspaper stand. As we passed by it, something caught Tadpole's eye and he stopped and reached for a display of disposable razors.

Just as I was about to advise him against shaving his tongue, a small headline near the bottom of the front page of *The Weekly Daily* caught my eye. It announced RED MENACE PAROLED. There was something awfully familiar about that name, and it suddenly came back to me that I had heard a number of older heroes mention it in passing recently. Given the slowness with which *The Weekly Daily* reported the news, I knew this parole could have happened a while ago.

"It's high time they let him out," the Inkblot spoke, interrupting my thoughts. "After all, he never really did any harm."

I glanced at the article. It stated that the Red Menace had been sentenced to 1,636 years in prison, but had just been paroled for good behavior after serving only fifty. Maybe I'm naive, but criminals who do no harm normally don't get put behind bars for 1,636 years.

"But just a couple of weeks ago, you told us he was one of the worst criminals in the history of the city," Plasma Girl pointed out. She was right—it was the Inkblot himself who had first mentioned the Red Menace to us the day we were here searching for one of the elusive Professor Brain-Drain collector cards.

"Oh, I'm sure I didn't say anything like that," scoffed the Inkblot. "The Red Menace only had good intentions when it came to the people of Superopolis."

"Then why does he have the word 'menace' in his name?" Halogen Boy asked with a perplexed look on his furry face.

The Inkblot glanced at him and the rest of our team, and a frown creased his face.

"The only menace to this city is young beatniks like you, with your crazy hair and far-out notions." The Inkblot raised his hands, fingers spread wide, and began waving them crazily. "Wild hair and wild ideas will be the ruin of society."

Well, he had a point about the hair. But before we could explain our run-in with Fuzz Boy, he continued with his rant.

"The Red Menace wanted to unite all Superopolis behind a single glorious vision, and with the help of Captain Radio, the greatest hero of my generation, he almost succeeded."

"But his plan was foiled, wasn't it?" I added.

"Yes, dabnab it," he replied, "by that consarned League of Goodness."

"But they're the real heroes," Stench insisted. "You thought so yourself just a couple weeks ago."

"He'th been brainwathed," Tadpole managed despite his hair-coated tongue.

Tadpole was right. Well, not about the Inkblot being *brainwathed*, but he most certainly had been *brainwashed*. It was a pattern that was becoming all too familiar.

I reached for my *Li'l Hero's Handbook*, and flipped to the Red Menace. I found an entry that described a villain who was the exact *opposite* of the hero that the Inkblot was attempting to portray. While the picture showed a somewhat younger man, there was no mistaking what I was seeing. The Red Menace and Comrade Crunch were one and the same.

NAME: Red Menace, The. **POWER:** Able to bend all to his will and compel them to do his bidding. **LIMITATIONS:** His power can be overcome by sound thinking and common sense, making him practically invincible. **CAREER:** His attempt at total domination was ultimately thwarted by the League of Goodness. **CLASSIFICATION:** One of the most dangerous villains ever.

CHAPTER FIVE

Chipth in Clath

When I got to school on Monday morning all my classmates were carrying cans of AI's Pseudo-Chips. They eagerly chatted among themselves, extolling the perfection of these stackable potato snacks.

"It'th a thientific fact that potato chipth tathte better when they're indithtinguithable from one another," Melonhead was asserting as I took my seat. No one was paying any attention to him.

"I can stack 'em up and eat fifteen at a time," Cannonball bragged as he proceeded to do just that.

"Now you can get even fatter in a fraction of the time," I pointed out.

Cannonball glared at me, but his mouth was so full of chips he couldn't respond.

"Look, I've arranged mine like the petals of a flower," Plasma Girl announced. Her chips were indeed laid out in a circle. Plucking one of the "petals" she raised it to her mouth. "I *do* love AI's Pseudo-Chips," she said popping the chip into her mouth. She instantly reached down for another. "I *don't* love AI's Pseudo-Chips," she declared, causing the class to let out a collective gasp before she ate that one as well.

"I *do* love AI's Pseudo-Chips," she repeated as she ate a third chip. The class let out a simultaneous sigh of relief. "I just don't know *why* I love them so much," she added in a low enough voice that only I heard.

Of course I knew why everyone loved them. It was because Comrade Crunch—I mean the Red Menace—had *everyone* in his power. Everyone, that is, except me. I was the only person I knew who hadn't gone head over heels for this bland new snack item. Sure, I had felt the lure of the Red Menace's power, but I always managed to break free of it.

"When did class time become snack time?" asked Miss Marble as she entered the room. There was almost always something that annoyed her first thing in the morning, and today it was a room full of kids munching on Pseudo-Chips.

"But they're irrethithtable, Mith Marble," Melonhead spattered. "I don't think I can go a thingle, tholitary thecond without them."

"I'd waste away to nothing," insisted Cannonball.

"Me, too," added Transparent Girl as she faded away to prove it.

"They make me stretchier," Limber Lass piped in.

"They make me sleepier." Somnia yawned as her head thunked onto her desk.

"And me bubblier!" Little Miss Bubbles giggled amid a bubbly eruption.

"What has gotten into you kids?" Miss Marble asked in exasperation. "The rules say no eating in class."

"Then let'th change the ruleth!" Melonhead slobbered.

"Melonhead is right!" Tadpole said to my astonishment. It was the first time in memory that anyone had ever listened to Melonhead, let alone agreed with him. That was all the encouragement the drooling doofus needed as he stood up in defiance.

"The majority thould dethide, and the majority wanth to have chipth in clath.

"Chipth in clath! Chipth in clath! Chipth in clath!" He began leading the entire class in a chant. Miss Marble was taken aback by it all and clearly didn't know how to respond. But as the Banshee joined in the ruckus with a high-pitched shriek, Miss Marble gathered her wits, and moments later the wailing and protesting was silenced as my classmates and I went as stiff as statues thanks to Miss Marble's power.

"I don't know what the big deal is with these chips," Miss Marble said.

Finally! Someone else who hadn't fallen under the sway of the Red Menace.

"But it's funny that you mention majority rules. You see, the planned lesson for this morning is on just that subject. You are correct that in a democracy the majority does indeed make the rules. Of course, the mistake you've made is assuming that when you're in school you're part of a democracy."

As she was saying this, she walked up and down the rows of desks plucking one canister of chips after another out of my classmates' unresisting grasps.

"You'll have plenty of time as adults to make moronic decisions in the voting booth. Politicians will lie outright to you and you'll believe them. They'll get caught, lie to you again, and you'll still turn around and reelect them. You'll vote for people not because they're competent or have your interests in mind, but because they have the same favorite color as you."

I would have considered this insulting if it weren't true. She was silent for a moment as she dumped all the chip canisters she had collected into the bottom drawer of her desk.

"People are naturally gullible and will believe almost anything they're told," she continued. "There is nothing I can teach you here that will change that sad fact. The Superopolis Board of Education has never thought it necessary to include lessons for their students on how not to be suckers."

The stiffness throughout my body began to fade.

"But what we *will* teach you is how this idiotic process works," she said sarcastically as motion slowly returned to my classmates. "With the upcoming mayoral election going on, it seems like a natural waste of time to stage our own class elections."

Despite his rigidity, Melonhead spotted an opportunity to promote himself, and creakily rose to his feet.

"If I'm chothen ath clath prethident, I'll change the ruleth to allow the Amathing Indethtructo'th Amathing Theudo-Chipth in thchool!"

"I nominate Melonhead as class president!" Cannonball announced even as he strained to elbow his best friend, Lobster Boy.

"Uh, I second the nomination," Lobster Boy said,

50

as he stiffly raised his claw to follow Cannonball's
lead.

"And he's nominating me for vice president,"
Cannonball added.

"I am?" Melonhead sputtered. He turned to look
at Cannonball, who glared at him threateningly. "Uh,
yeah, I gueth I'm nominating Cannonball ath my running mate."

After another elbow from Cannonball, Lobster Boy
seconded the nomination.

"Melonhead as class president?!" Tadpole uttered
in disgust. Apparently, he had gotten over his earlier
moment of support. "That would be
a disaster."

I agreed, especially with
Cannonball on the same
ticket. There was only one
solution.

"I nominate Tadpole
for president,"
I shouted.
Plasma Girl
immediately
seconded the
nomination.

"I'll run for

vice president," volunteered the Spore eagerly. No one paid any attention, and a moment later, we chose Plasma Girl as Tadpole's running mate.

"Very good." Miss Marble clucked approvingly. "But none of you really needs to worry about whom actually wins. The class president has no power whatsoever—not that it will stop any of you from thinking that this is the most important election of your lives."

She was right about that. The rest of the period was taken up with choosing candidates for other meaningless offices. Transparent Girl joined Melonhead's ticket as their candidate for class treasurer, a position that would oversee the class fish food fund. At the moment it consisted of a jelly jar that held exactly twenty-three cents and two pencil stubs. To my surprise, Stench nominated me as our party's candidate for the post.

The Spore had volunteered both times to be treasurer, but everyone ignored him.

We then added Little Miss Bubbles as our nominee for secretary, a job that involved doing absolutely nothing as far as any of us could tell. The Spore raised his hand frantically in an attempt to be nominated as the opposing candidate, but Cannonball didn't even see him. Instead, he nominated Somnia for that vital role while she dozed at her desk unaware. Somnia's ability to put people to sleep made her the perfect candidate for this position.

"So we have our candidates," Miss Marble said.

"What about me?" wailed the Spore, looking like he might undergo meiosis.

"There are no other offices to fill," she apologized.

"Nothing?" he wailed as Miss Marble looked exasperated.

"Oh, fine," she finally answered. "You can run for . . . class coroner."

The rest of the class was shocked, but the Spore couldn't have been more pleased. Needless to say, no one wanted to run against him for that office.

With the slates all set, we gathered into groups to develop campaign strategies. By the time the bell rang for recess, the excitement of a class election was in full swing.

It wasn't until after we all left the room that I realized I hadn't asked Miss Marble how she and I appeared to be the only people not affected by the commands of the Red Menace. I turned around to go back into the classroom but came to a sudden halt in the doorway. Unaware of my presence, Miss Marble had opened up her bottom drawer and retrieved one of

NAME: Spore, The. **POWER:** Wherever he goes, mold and mildew are sure to follow. **LIMITATIONS:** Antibiotics could prove fatal. **CAREER:** A budding entrepreneur, the Spore has an unerring nose for sniffing out truffles. **CLASSIFICATION:** A tendency by others to mistake him for being dead could prove problematic for future success.

the confiscated canisters. She was eagerly and happily stuffing the chips into her mouth.

"Irresistible," I heard her mumble faintly to herself as she chewed.

CHAPTER SIX

Transparency in Government

The second half of the day dragged on as Miss Marble described the electoral process until even I was thoroughly bored.

"And so the candidate with the most money then buys the most ads and thus wins the race," she concluded. "And I assume that's the way it's always been."

"Miss Marble?"

"Yes, Ordinary Boy," Miss Marble responded in a way that indicated I was throwing her off her lecture plan.

"You said you assumed that's how it's always been," I pointed out. "Can we talk about history for just a second?"

"Why would we do that?" she responded with

annoyance. "It's all in the past."

"O Boy is just trying to keep us from focusing on the election," Transparent Girl piped up. "He knows his side is going to get creamed."

"Maybe if we look at things that happened in the past, they can give us answers to events that are occurring right now," I proposed, ignoring my opponent.

"So what exactly is it that you're curious about?" asked a skeptical Miss Marble.

"I'd like to know what you can tell us about the Red Menace," I said.

"The Red Menace?" Miss Marble responded as if she hadn't heard the name in decades. "The Red Menace is a villain who went away when I was half your age. What could you possibly need to know about him?"

"He's free now," I informed her, "and I think it might be important to know something about him."

"Well if he's free, the Superopolis Parole Board obviously thought it was safe to release him," she said. "End of story. Now let's get back to discussing the election."

"I have something very important I need to tell everyone regarding the election," Transparent Girl blurted out. Miss Marble happily took the opportunity to move on from my questioning.

"Certainly, Transparent Girl." She nodded. "You have the floor."

"As your candidate for treasurer," she began as she

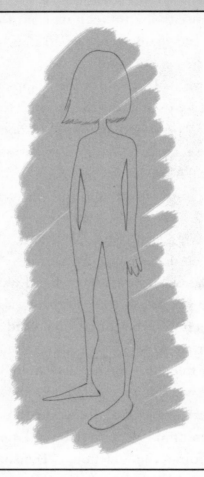

NAME: Transparent Girl. **POWER:** The ability to make herself nearly invisible. **LIMITATIONS:** She always leaves a partial outline. **CAREER:** With motives as transparent as she is herself, we expect her future goals to be readily apparent to all. **CLASSIFICATION:** You can see right through her.

rose to her feet, "I think it's my duty to alert you all to the fiscal crisis that is brewing right beneath our noses."

We all glanced down to see if there was anything beneath our noses, but found only our desks. Transparent Girl was up to something, and I glanced up at her semitranslucent form as I tried to figure out what it might be.

"Our class treasury," she continued, "has been completely depleted thanks to the financial incompetence of my opponent, Ordinary Boy."

"What??!!" I shot up from my seat. "I'm not the treasurer. We don't even have one yet."

"Miss Marble," she huffed as she became even more transparent, "I believe I have the floor."

"You do"—Miss Marble frowned—"but you better be careful how you use it if you're going to make accusations like that."

"It's true," she insisted. "Just this afternoon, I came back from recess and found our fish food fund completely empty—robbed of everything it contained."

"I didn't take it!" I fumed.

"I never said you did," she said as she faded to just a vague outline. "But isn't it true that you did nothing to prevent the theft?"

"Neither did you," I shot back.

"On the contrary," she responded smugly, "I am now doing everything I can to prevent you from causing further harm by getting *myself* elected class treasurer."

Just as I was about to blow up again, I spotted the coins in her pocket. Unlike her, they had not faded at all. There was exactly twenty-three cents, plus two pencil stubs.

"What's more," she went on as I began to point and sputter, "if elected, I will create a new fund with money raised by selling all our schoolbooks to buy more cans of AI's Pseudo-Chips."

The class erupted into cheers as I sank into my seat in frustration.

"Meanwhile, my opponent"—Transparent Girl went in for the kill—"doesn't even *like* Pseudo-Chips."

The shocked and disapproving silence from my classmates was interrupted only by the final bell. With Transparent Girl's charges unanswered we filed from class. I was fuming at how this had all been turned against me. How was I going to recover from her charges?

"So are you going to come with us?" asked Plasma Girl.

"Huh?" I responded, jolted out of my train of thought. "Come with you where?"

"We were saying that we wanted to go to the Mighty Mart," she said.

"Yeah," agreed Stench. "Miss Marble took all our Pseudo-Chips and we need to buy more."

"Maybe if you get some, too, they'll help keep you focused," Tadpole suggested. "Everyone knows that they sharpen the mind."

"That's the dumbest thing I've ever heard." I snorted. "They're potato chips—and barely even that!—not some kind of miracle food."

My friends stared at me as if I had made some unforgivable comment.

"Fine," Plasma Girl said with a sniff after an uncomfortable pause. "Don't come with us."

As they turned to head for the Mighty Mart, I felt like I was about to lose my best friends. Until I knew what the Red Menace was up to, I needed to give my teammates the benefit of the doubt.

"I'm sorry, guys," I said. "It's not right of me to make fun of something that you all like. I'll come along with you and I promise to stop insulting AI's chips—as long as I can still keep insulting AI himself."

"Do as much of that as you want," Halogen Boy said with a grin.

When we got to the Mighty Mart, the place was mobbed with customers, and they were all there for one purpose—to buy even more of the Amazing Indestructo's Amazing Pseudo-Chips. My friends rushed off to do likewise.

Having no interest in Pseudo-Chips, I wandered over to one of the aisles that held the entire Dr. Telomere's line to pick out some *real* chips for myself. I arrived just as the last jumbo-size bags of Dr. Telomere's X-tra Crispy Potato Chips were being boxed up.

"What happened to all the Dr. Telomere's?" I asked incredulously as I grabbed the final two bags off the shelf. Mr. Mister, the store manager, was supervising the switchover and turned around at my comment.

"Nobody wants any of those relics of the past." He sniffed dismissively as a fine spray of moisture drifted down onto my head.

"I do!" I blurted out.

"Well, I'm afraid you're out of luck," he replied. "You seem to be the only one who wants them. The Dr. Telomere's factory has already ceased production, and we're dumping what we have in order to make room for more Pseudo-Chips."

I glared up at Mr. Mister. I assumed he was equally irritated with me based on the amount of mist that was gathering around his head. Before I could say

something I shouldn't, I heard a familiar voice from the next aisle over.

"But how can I *not* tell people how incredible they are?"

"Dad?" I followed my father's voice to the snack cake aisle where he was stationed in front of a huge display of Maximizer Brand products. Only he wasn't holding any Maximizer cakes but rather a can of Amazing Indestructo Pseudo-Chips. His boss, the Great Garbanzo, was standing there, too, and he clearly wasn't happy.

"I don't gives a monkey's butt how much youse likes dem chips," fumed the giant chickpea. "Youse guys woik for me, not de Amazin' Indestructo."

"But nobody is buying anything but Pseudo-Chips," my dad insisted. "Nobody's even paying attention to us."

"Den clearlies I hired myself de wrong team a heroes." The Great Garbanzo dropped his voice to a menacing level. I just knew this wasn't going to be good. "So it's times I gets myself a new one. Youse, and yer whole team, is FIRED!"

The expression of surprise on my father's face turned to utter humiliation as he looked over and saw that I had witnessed the whole thing.

CHAPTER SEVEN

When the Chips Are Down

My dad put on a brave face as we walked home, but I could tell he was devastated at having been fired. That it had happened in front of me just made it a hundred times worse.

"It's not really a big deal, Dad," I said. "Everybody is spending so much of their money on Pseudo-Chips that nobody has any left to spend on Maximizer snack cakes, anyway."

"Maximizer *Brand* snack cakes," he replied out of force of habit. "But we finally had an endorsement deal. Do you know how hard they are to get?"

"I know. But the Great Garbanzo is a jerk," I said. "Even worse. He's a *joik!*"

That got a small laugh out of my dad.

"Something will come along," I continued. "Besides, it's not like you'd be any better off if you'd remained at Dr. Telomere's. They're out of business entirely."

"I never thought I'd see the day." My father sighed as he shook his head.

"How long has the company been around?" I asked.

"Forever." He shrugged. "Or at least for as long as I can remember. Dr. Telomere's chips have just always been there."

"Until now," I concluded his thought. "But who owns the company, anyway? Is there really a Dr. Telomere?"

"Oh, no." My dad laughed—this time a little more genuinely. "Dr. Telomere is just a marketing character. Look at the bag."

I pulled out one of the bags of Dr. Telomere's X-tra Crispy Chips that I had managed to buy. Framed in a circle, within the overall brand logo, was a smiling potato chip wearing pince-nez glasses, a bow tie, and a derby. He was winking as if he were sharing a secret with me.

"That's Dr. Telomere." My father chuckled. "Does he look like he could be a real person?"

DR. TELOMERE

Despite his fragile nature, Dr. Telomere is one potato chip that has long avoided being crushed or consumed. Earlier, more realistic versions of the popular advertising icon have steadily changed over the decades into the simple cartoon figure everyone is familiar with today. Despite once being able to sing and dance, the character has been mute now for some time, making it impossible to glean any of the secrets he may possess.

Considering that Dad had just been fired by a guy who looked like a giant chickpea, I wasn't certain that the answer to that question was so obvious.

"Who owns the business, then?" I prodded.

"The Telomere Trust," my dad said as we continued to walk. "It's a fund that uses the profits from the business to pay for things for the community."

"Like Telomere Park," I said.

"Exactly. The Telomere Trust has done all sorts of good things for the people of Superopolis."

"I'm sure the Amazing Indestructo is going to be equally generous with his profits," I suggested sarcastically.

"He's going to make a fortune," my father agreed with a sigh. "How could he not with such a phenomenal product."

I cringed as Dad retrieved one of the cans of Pseudo-Chips we had also bought, popped off the lid, and started eating them. How was I going to break him free from the Red Menace's hold? As we arrived home, I remembered that he wasn't the only one I was going to have to rescue. My mom was in the driveway with her own grocery bags full of Pseudo-Chips.

"Thermo! OB!" she shouted. "You're just in time to help me unload the rest of my groceries. I found a roadside stand on my way home that was selling Pseudo-Chips. I figured we could use some more."

There had to be another hundred cans of chips in the car. With a shrug of resignation, I grabbed a few bags and helped my parents haul them into the house. Dad had put on a big phony smile and I realized that he wasn't ready yet to tell Mom what had just happened to his endorsement deal. I gave him a wink to let him know that she wouldn't hear it from me.

"How was work, Mom?" I asked.

"Oh, the usual," was all she said.

I've never understood exactly what my mom does at the Corpsicle Coolant Corporation. Whenever I ask, she always just says something about frozen vegetables, which usually is enough to end the conversation.

As I set the bags of chips down on our kitchen counter, I actually hoped we *would* be having some frozen vegetables tonight. The thought of a meal of only Pseudo-Chips wasn't a pleasant one. But that was apparently what was on the menu as

Mom poured an entire can into a bowl for my father and then another for herself. As she reached for a third, presumably for me, I stopped her.

"I'll just have these," I said, holding up one of my bags of Dr. Telomere's.

My parents looked at me as if I had just announced I was quitting school to become a mime. Unsure how to respond, they grudgingly let me proceed. We all sat down at the dinner table with our preferred brands of chips. There was an uncomfortable silence that I decided to break with a question I had been trying to get an answer to all day.

"Mom? Dad?" I began. "Do either of you know anything about the Red Menace?"

"Is that a brand of chewing gum?" my father asked. "It's cinnamony, isn't it?"

I shook my head as both he and Mom stared at each other blankly. It was beginning to dawn on me that nobody in this city had much knowledge or interest in history—unless it directly involved *them* somehow.

"He's a villain," I supplied them the answer. "He was put in prison fifty years ago and they've just let him out."

"Well, that was nice of the city," my mom responded. "He must be very old by now and obviously can't cause any harm. What is his power?"

"He can convince people to do anything he wants them to do," I said looking them directly in the eyes. Their vacant expressions told me that I hadn't gotten my point across. "Like switch to a new kind of potato chip, even if it isn't any good," I added.

"Well, he'll never get anywhere with that." My dad laughed. "No one could ever convince people to switch from AI's Amazing Pseudo-Chips."

I dropped my head in exasperation. How was I going to convince my parents that Comrade Crunch/the Red Menace was up to no good? I finished off the small bowl of potato chips in front of me and then excused myself.

"I think I need to go up to my room and lie down for a while," I announced, only partly feigning exhaustion.

The truth was, I was completely baffled. What was going on with the Red Menace and AI's Pseudo-Chips? I went into my room and flopped onto the bed. Absentmindedly, I picked up a knitting needle that was sitting on my nightstand. It was my one souvenir from my recent trip back in time, and I began tapping it against the side of my head as I thought things through.

What had me flustered was the realization that the Red Menace hadn't broken any laws. He had been paroled from jail, and the Amazing Indestructo had

71

legitimately hired him to promote his new line of potato chips. There wasn't anything prohibiting the Red Menace from using his power to advertise a product. Single-handedly driving Superopolis's most successful company out of business might not have been nice, but it wasn't illegal.

Clearly this had to be a far tamer use of his power than the events of fifty years ago that got him sent to prison for 1,636 years. But what had he done to deserve that sentence in the first place? I needed to know more about him. If only there was someone I could turn to for information.

And then it hit me—literally. I stopped tapping the knitting needle against my head and looked at it. Not only did I know the person best able to reveal the Red Menace's criminal past but I also had the perfect excuse to pay him a visit.

CHAPTER EIGHT

On Pins and Needles

"Okay, I know you guys think I'm overreacting about the Red Menace," I said to my friends as we left school the next day. "But I think there's someone who can give us all the information we need about him."

"If you're talking about *Comrade Crunch*, I don't know what your problem is," Tadpole replied stubbornly.

"Yeah, O Boy," agreed Stench. "We know you don't like the Pseudo-Chips, but that's no reason to believe that Comrade Crunch is up to anything evil."

"That's not all . . ." Plasma Girl started to speak but then hesitated. She glanced nervously at the other members of the team.

"What is it?" I demanded. Clearly there was something they were afraid to tell me.

"Well," she continued haltingly, "it's just that *every-one* loves AI's Pseudo-Chips—except you."

"And?" I pressed.

"Everyone thinks there's something strange about you because of it," Halogen Boy added softly.

"And it's messing up our chances in the election," Tadpole felt compelled to add.

I was struck silent for a moment. All my life people had thought of me as different—for the simple reason that I *am* different. My lack of a power had marked me that way from birth. But I'd had years to get used to it, and so had my friends. So the fact that even they were now expressing doubt really hurt.

"Fine," I said as calmly as I could. "Just come with me and keep an open mind. If you still feel that way after our next stop, I'll concede the point."

"Where exactly are we going?" Hal asked.

"We're going to visit the leader of the League of Goodness," I announced as I produced the knitting needle I had been keeping in my backpack all day.

"The Amazing Indestructo?!" they all exclaimed in unison.

"Why would he do anything to help us?" Plasma Girl said in exasperation.

"And when did he take up knitting?" asked Hal.

"Not the leader of the League of *Ultimate*

74

Goodness," I corrected them. "I'm talking about the original League of Goodness—before AI took control and turned the group into a bunch of bungling bone-heads. We're going to go see Lord Pincushion."

My teammates had never been officially introduced to the legendary hero, and were excited to meet him. Their mood improved dramatically as I led them to the base of Needlepoint Hill.

"How are we going to get up there?" Tadpole asked as his eyes followed the thousands of stairs that criss-crossed their way up the hill to the mansion that sat atop it. "It would take forever to climb it."

Tadpole was right, of course. I had climbed it myself just a week earlier. Since then, I had learned of a simpler way.

"Follow me," I said as I led them around to the other side of the hill. There, partly obscured behind some bushes and trees, was an elevator door. Once inside I pressed the button for the main entrance to Pinprick Manor.

The car rose quickly up the interior of Needlepoint Hill. When it finally came to a stop, the doors opened to reveal a beautifully wood-paneled foyer. And standing there waiting for us was the founder of the League of Goodness himself.

"Good heavens, it's Ordinary Boy," he said as a

smile spread across his face. "I do hope you're not here to disrupt the fabric of space and time again."

"Not today." I returned his smile. "I've come to return something that belongs to you."

"Indeed?" he responded as I held out the knitting needle I had borrowed less than a week ago, my time, but over twenty-five years ago for him. "I was wondering what had happened to that." Taking the needle from me he examined it briefly and then jammed it into the front of his thigh. My friends' eyes went wide with alarm. Lord Pincushion caught their surprised reactions. "And who are these young heroes?"

"These are my teammates, the Junior Leaguers," I said. "Stench, Tadpole, Halogen Boy, and Plasma Girl."

"Charmed, I'm sure," Lord Pincushion responded as he stuck out his hand to each of them. One at a time they maneuvered around an array of thumbtacks, needles, fishing hooks, and finishing nails to gingerly shake his hand.

"And now I must insist on entertaining you all properly." He smiled at us. "Follow me to the library, please. I believe we'll find the Animator there."

The Animator had also been an original member of the League of Goodness and was now retired as well. As our host led the way, we fell in behind, staring at the magnificence of Pinprick Manor. It was hard to imagine that such a large mansion was home to only two people.

"You'll have to excuse us," our host apologized as he led us down one of the long corridors and stopped in front of a large double door. "It's cleaning day, so things could be a bit messy."

No sooner had he swung open the door than a swarm of books flew past us, flapping their covers and pages as if they were birds. Once inside, we saw there were literally thousands of them soaring and circling their away around the enormous room. In the process, clouds of dust were being shaken free and then sucked into a large, flat, spinning disk of debris floating midair in the center of the room. Within the rotating swirl, the particles were coalescing into one giant ball just like a miniature galaxy.

Below the disk, dancing merrily around to his own internal music of the cosmos, was the Animator. As he sent one flock of aired-out books back to their shelves he immediately directed another bay of dusty tomes to burst from their bookcase. My friends and I all watched the marvelous sight with our mouths agape.

"We're dusting the books today," Lord Pincushion

observed rather dryly, not quite sharing our awe.

Soon the number of books winging their way around the room began to thin, and as the last of the flapping volumes shook themselves clean, the elderly superhero focused his attention on the spinning galaxy of dust. It turned faster and faster, and the debris was pulled toward the center, where it formed into a solid, rotating orb of dirt. When no loose particles remained, the Animator raised his left hand toward the spinning sphere and it burst into flames like a sun flaring to life.

"Whoa!" we all said as we turned our heads away. The brilliant light didn't last long, however, as the fire quickly consumed the giant dust ball and then winked out of existence. My friends and I began to clap.

"My goodness," the Animator said in surprise, just noticing our presence. "Is that Ordinary Boy? What a pleasure to see you again, lad!"

"And you," I replied. "That's quite a cleaning system you have."

"I do what I can to make it enjoyable," the Animator admitted. "Dusting the books is so much more fun than say . . . cleaning the bathroom."

"He tried the same method there, once," Lord Pincushion confided to me, "but it looked more like a giant flushing toilet, I'm afraid."

"Ah, well, who wants to talk about cleaning when we have guests." The Animator clapped his hands. "Let's sit down and I'll get us some refreshments."

Our hosts ushered us over to a corner of the library where a number of chairs were situated around a large coffee table. No sooner had we sat down than two empty suits of armor entered the library. One held a tray bearing seven empty glasses and two pitchers of lemonade. The other carried a tray with one large bowl filled with potato chips along with several empty smaller bowls.

This wasn't our first encounter with the silent servants of Pinprick Manor. I had met them on my first visit, and my friends had been introduced to them when they helped us in our battle with dinosaurs the previous week in Telomere Park.

More surprising than an animated suit of armor, however, was the large bowl of potato chips they carried. These were genuine, honest-to-goodness Dr. Telomere's potato chips. As Lord Pincushion and the Animator took their seats, I eagerly took one of the smaller bowls and filled it up with chips from the larger. A moment later I realized how rude I must have seemed, but that was nothing compared to my friends' behavior.

"Um . . ." Stench started to say, as he spoke for the

others, "would you mind if we ate our own chips?"

Tadpole opened his backpack and retrieved a can of Amazing Indestructo's Pseudo-Chips. Plasma Girl reached for four of the smaller bowls as Tadpole opened the canister. He then poured a portion of the chips into each bowl.

"Good heavens, what *are* those?" Lord Pincushion said with surprise. To my relief, he had obviously not seen any of the Red Menace's ads.

"This is why we're here," I admitted. "It's these chips. They've completely pushed Dr. Telomere's chips off the market. That's why I was so excited to see you still had some."

"Of course we do. We have several weeks' supply at any given time," explained Lord Pincushion as both he and his partner took one of the Pseudo-Chips.

"How could *these* have replaced Dr. Telomere's?" asked the Animator as he took a bite. "They taste like baked napkins."

"It's not the chips," I explained. "It's AI's new spokesman. He's on the air constantly."

"Is he now." Lord Pincushion bristled with irritation. "Well let's just get a look at him."

Before I could stop him, our host pressed a button on the arm of his chair. Directly across from us a wall cabinet swung open revealing an old-fashioned television set, which immediately burst to life. Lord Pincushion's timing couldn't have been worse, for there on the screen was the Red Menace extolling the benefits of AI's Pseudo-Chips.

". . . that's right. Reach for an Amazing Indestructo's Amazing Pseudo-Chip right this very minute. Go ahead, you know you want—"

I jumped up and shut off the TV, but as I turned and saw the blank stares on the faces of the Animator and Lord Pincushion, I feared the damage had already been done.

CHAPTER NINE

The Rise of the Red Menace

As Lord Pincushion reached for another Pseudo-Chip, I was certain that he, too, had fallen under the sway of the Red Menace. But then to my surprise, he crushed the chip in his hand.

"So he's back," he stated grimly. "Fifty years after we put the Red Menace away, society has decided to let him out. It's an error they will come to regret."

"I know he's up to something," I agreed, "but no one believes me. Not even my friends."

My teammates looked at one another guiltily.

"It's not their fault," said the Animator. "The Red Menace has a powerful ability. But he isn't infallible."

"Indeed," agreed Lord Pincushion. "Whatever he's

up to, he *can* be beaten. We proved it ourselves fifty years ago."

"What exactly happened then?" I asked eagerly.

"It's quite a story," the Animator said and then tipped his head to his partner to do the telling.

"It was a simpler time," Lord Pincushion began. "The modern age was dawning, yet people's lives had not yet been consumed by technology. Things that now seem mundane to you children were the scientific marvels of the day. And chief among these wonders was the miracle of radio."

"Radio?!" Tadpole snorted. "But it doesn't even have pictures."

"The pictures were here, boy," Lord Pincushion bristled. He was pointing to a corncob spear stuck in his temple, but I presume he meant his head.

"Our imaginations provided the images. There was a hero then who was master of this new technology and he towered above the rest. His name was Captain Radio."

I sat up, keenly interested. I remembered the Inkblot once described Captain Radio as the Amazing Indestructo of his day.

"Captain Radio had complete control over the radio waves," the Animator interjected. "That was his power."

"That's correct." Lord Pincushion nodded. "Not

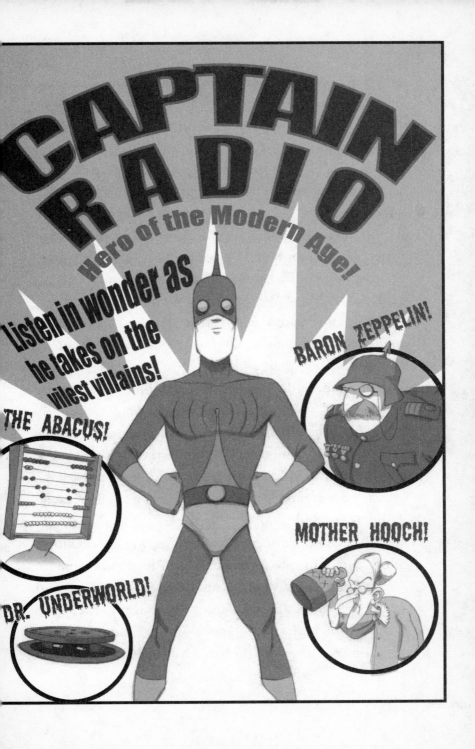

only was he able to ride the radio waves through the air, he was also able to transport himself instantaneously from one end of Superopolis to the other across those waves."

"Wow!" Stench said in awe. "So he could be anywhere at any time! That had to be a huge plus for a superhero."

"It was," Lord Pincushion agreed. "But even that aspect of Captain Radio's power paled in comparison to another facet of his talent—the ability to promote himself."

"Captain Radio could trumpet his accomplishments across the same radio waves he traveled upon," the Animator explained.

"Indeed," added Lord Pincushion. "He was the first hero to have the means to communicate directly with the general population. And in broadcasting his own adventures, he was able to give the public only the version of his exploits that he wanted them to hear."

"I never missed an episode of his show," the Animator added fondly.

"Of course we were only hearing the good things, and we bought into all of it." Lord Pincushion sighed. "We weren't as savvy as you children are today, and Captain Radio attained a celebrity that no other hero before him had ever come close to achieving. His ubiquitous presence and his self-broadcasted exploits made him a household name. It was a new concept in the hero business that no one else matched—until the arrival of that unfortunate Indestructo."

I knew that any talk of AI could put Lord Pincushion in a cranky mood, so I attempted to redirect the story.

"But what about the Red Menace?" I asked. "How does this relate to him?"

"Ah, this is but a mere prelude, son." Lord Pincushion's expression softened again. "I needed to give you a sense of the world in which the Red Menace first made his appearance.

"As you are all too well aware, the Red Menace possesses the ability to manipulate people to obey his every command. This is a dangerous power in anyone's hands, but in the case of the Red Menace it was a catastrophe."

"Why so?" Plasma Girl asked.

"Because the Red Menace hated capitalism. He thought that no one should have to work and that everything should be shared equally. He even believed that there should be no laws in society and that every-one should be allowed to do exactly as he pleased."

"Sounds good to me," Tadpole interjected.

"Many people think so." Lord Pincushion sniffed dismissively. "At least until one person's freedom to do as he pleases interferes with another's. Of course in the end the Red Menace instituted his own laws and forced everyone to live by his rules, and his rules only."

"Yet in the beginning his message—backed by his power—had appeal," added the Animator.

"There was just one problem," Lord Pincushion continued. "The Red Menace couldn't get his ideas out. Converting people one at a time or even in small groups was ineffective."

"Right," I piped in. "The people he converted didn't possess his power, so they couldn't pass his commands along to others. His message had no way of spreading on its own."

"Correct." The Animator beamed. "You're a bright boy!"

I blushed as my friends smirked at me.

"Exactly," added Lord Pincushion pointedly. "But then he met Captain Radio and everything changed. The Red Menace used his power to gain control of Captain Radio, and then used the captain's ability to broadcast his commands. The power in his voice was just as effective over the airwaves as it was in person, and the majority of the populace quickly fell under his sway."

"Just as they have now, thanks to his TV commercials," I added.

"Wait a minute," Tadpole interrupted. "Are you saying I've fallen in love with these new potato chips just because some guy is using his power on me?

That's despicable! I can make my own decisions."

What Lord Pincushion said had hit at the heart of Tadpole's ego—the belief that *he* was the only one responsible for his actions. I could practically see the gears turning in his head as he got more and more steamed.

"And there you have the simple secret to thwarting the Red Menace's power," concluded Lord Pincushion. "Thinking for yourself can overcome anyone's attempt to manipulate you—even if it *is* his power. Some people are intelligent enough to never let themselves be taken in," he said, looking at me, "while others merely need to be shown the light."

My teammates considered the Pseudo-Chips in front of them. Then Halogen Boy pushed his bowl to the far end of the coffee table.

"They really do taste like sawdust," Stench added, pushing his bowl away as well. "I feel like an idiot."

"No, son," said the Animator kindly, "an idiot is a person who is shown the truth but refuses to believe it."

"Yes," agreed Lord Pincushion. "There will always be people who are more concerned with stubbornly holding on to a failed belief than admitting an error. There are no greater fools. Happily, you children are not among them."

"I'm embarrassed that I fell for it at all," Plasma Girl admitted.

"Don't be," Lord Pincushion reassured her. "The Red Menace has a formidable power."

"And now you all know *how* he is able to do what he does," added the Animator.

"Yet the bigger question remains unanswered," Lord Pincushion said with concern. "Exactly *why* is he doing it?"

CHAPTER TEN

A Parade of Lies

What *was* the Red Menace up to? The question that Lord Pincushion had left us with yesterday had been gnawing at me ever since. Near the end of class on Wednesday, I still hadn't come up with an answer. On the bright side, at least things hadn't gotten any worse in my race for treasurer. Transparent Girl had been unusually quiet all day. I should have known it wouldn't last. . . .

Ten minutes before the final bell the Banshee let out a piercing wail.

"Miss Marble!!" she shrieked as we all cringed and covered our ears. "Fingold is dead!"

Fingold was one of the two dozen or so fish in our aquarium. This watery tragedy wasn't exactly a unique occurrence. Our fish routinely took that one-way float to the top of the tank. In fact, part of our fish food fund often went toward buying replacements. Only now the fund was empty, and I knew that if I didn't speak first, Transparent Girl—

"Miss Marble!" she hollered before I could beat her to it. "Tragedy is upon us. But far be it for me to cast any blame."

As she said it, her form took on enough solidity so that everyone in the class could see her arm outstretched, her finger pointing directly at me.

Everyone turned and looked at me as if I had used my own hands to strangle the life out of poor Fingold. As I sputtered to defend myself, the Spore got up from his seat and walked somberly back to the aquarium. He retrieved the body with a small net and laid it out in an empty pencil case.

"Fingold—" he huffed as he practiced for his role as coroner "—is . . . dead."

Somnia lowered her head in respect and quickly fell asleep. The sound of her forehead clunking against her desk distracted me just enough for my opponent to pounce.

"But he won't be forgotten," Transparent Girl announced. "Which is why I'm proud to announce, in honor of our fallen fishy friend, the formation of the Fingold Memorial Fish Fund for the financing of fishes forever." She paused for dramatic effect. "And I will make the first donation myself."

Even as she said it, she made her way back to the empty jelly jar, into which she proceeded to deposit the same twenty-three cents and two pencil stubs that she had taken on Monday.

"So while my opponent favors the death of fish," Transparent Girl concluded, "I am starting this fund to help save them."

Things only got worse from there. No matter

what I said to defend myself, Transparent Girl found a way to turn it against me. By the time the bell finally rang, I wasn't sure that *I* would have voted for myself.

"Man, we don't stand a chance," Tadpole grumped as we all filed out of the school. "Nobody is going to vote for us."

"I'm sorry, guys," I said with a sigh. "Maybe it would be best if I just dropped out of the race so I don't sink our entire ticket."

"It's not your fault, O Boy," Plasma Girl said, just as Tadpole was looking like he was about to accept my offer. "People will eventually see through Transparent Girl."

"Don't they already?" Halogen Boy cocked his head in confusion.

"See through what she's *saying*," Plasma Girl corrected.

"I hope so," I said as we left the school grounds and headed north. "But that issue is really pretty minor compared to the Red Menace. How are we ever going to convince people to see through what *he's* saying?"

"Yeah, what exactly is our plan to bring down that crazy old nutcase?" Tadpole asked as we approached Colossal Way, the main road connecting the western part of the city to downtown.

"Lord Pincushion said it's important for us to find out what he's up to," Stench reminded us.

It was a relief to know that at least my friends no longer thought I was nuts. They were now equally convinced that the Red Menace was somehow living up to his name.

"But how do we do that?" Plasma Girl asked just as we reached Colossal Way. "We don't even know where to find him."

The words were barely out of her mouth when we turned the corner and discovered an enormous parade making its way toward us. At the head of it was the Red Menace himself.

As it got closer we saw that the parade was actually just a single float. It was a large, flat motorized vehicle that looked like a giant Pseudo-Chip. Major Bummer was in the driver's seat. Perched on a tall stand behind him, and surrounded by other members of the League of Ultimate Goodness, was the Red Menace. He was talking into a bullhorn so that everyone could hear his voice.

"That's right, citizens of Superopolis," he announced. "Express your collective will by following me to the Telomere Chip Factory."

The rest of the "parade" was just a massive crowd of

people following obediently behind the Red Menace.

"There I will convince all those who used to make that inferior brand of potato chips to instead come to work making the future of potato-y goodness," he continued. "They'll follow the path to Pseudo-Chip perfection!"

The crowd went wild, and every person the float passed joined the parade to Dr. Telomere's. As it got to us, however, we forced ourselves to stay put. Well, in truth, Halogen Boy started to move toward the crowd, but Plasma Girl had grabbed him by his cape and yanked him back to the side of the road.

"We feel it, too," she had told Hal, "but just keep telling yourself he's trying to manipulate us."

Despite the hypnotic tug of the Red Menace's words, we all stayed where we were. The only problem was that our unusual behavior attracted some attention.

"Hey, kids," shouted the Crimson Creampuff from aboard the float. "Hop on the bandwagon and come along with us. Everybody loves AI's Pseudo-Chips."

"It's true," added Featherweight as he wafted over to us. "They're crisp, they're flavorful, you can stack 'em like a deck of cards, and—" A breeze whisked him away before he could pile on even more one-sided comments.

NAME: Featherweight. **POWER:** He's literally the weight of a feather. **LIMITATIONS:** Has a hard time keeping his feet on the ground. **CAREER:** Could never hold down a job until he drifted to the attention of the Amazing Indestructo. **CLASSIFICATION:** Brings new meaning to the term "lightweight."

"And don't-a forget that Pseudo-Chips, they help-a keep us free," Spaghetti Man pointed out.

"How do they do that?" I asked skeptically. "They're just chips. And they don't taste anywhere near as good as Dr. Telomere's."

"Aaarghh, sonny," Cap'n Blowhole interjected. "Those landlubbin' chips are just all wet."

"Goodness gracious, what's makin' you young uns say such things?" asked Whistlin' Dixie, having moseyed over to see what the fuss was all about. "Don't y'all know that Pseudo-Chips are made fer regular old plain folks like you and me?"

"Yah, and I svear by zem," added Mannequin. "Zey help keep my skin zmooth and zupple."

We were getting the hard sell from the League of Ultimate Goodness, but it was about to get worse.

"Everybody loves Pseudo-Chips," another, more compelling voice rose above the rest.

The LUGs all moved aside to reveal the Red Menace as he stepped off the float and came over to face us. For the first time I was seeing him close up and I was struck by how old he was.

"The rest of you can continue to the factory," he instructed the members of the league.

As they did so, the parade moved ahead, now under the much less compelling direction of Major Bummer.

"I don't know about you," the Major sighed into the bullhorn, "but whenever I think of Dr. Telomere's chips, I get so depressed." And so did the crowd as his mood was transferred to them.

"Why don't you children want to come along with lovable old Comrade Crunch?" the Red Menace asked with a calculating smile as he approached us in his role as Superopolis's favorite grandfatherly figure.

"We're not interested in him," I replied, despite a strong urge to find him "lovable." "But we *are* interested in the Red Menace."

"Aha!" he said to my surprise as his smile changed to one of genuine delight. "So I haven't been forgotten. I was beginning to think that no one but a few old codgers remembered who I was. And even as I encounter those few who do, I find myself needing to remind them of how much good I did for the city of Superopolis."

So that explained the Inkblot's altered views on the Red Menace.

"Nobody seems to remember much about the past," I stated, "let alone what you tried to do."

"That's why I'm back." The Red Menace's eyes narrowed as he viewed me with suspicion. "To complete the task that was interrupted all those years ago— the task of bringing order and equality to everyone. It's a noble task, don't you agree?"

"Those sound like good things," Stench said almost robotically as the villain's full power was unleashed on us. I forced myself to resist it.

"No, I don't agree," I shot back. The Red Menace recoiled as if I had struck him.

"So you can resist my power," he sneered. "There have always been a few people who can. But it doesn't really matter. My plan is moving forward and nothing is going to stop it."

"What plan?" I pressed. "What are you trying to do?"

"It's all right in front of you." He swept his hand to indicate the crowd of followers as they continued to move along. "The people are helping me with my quest to make everybody perfect by first making every potato chip perfect. It's an apt metaphor."

"What do you mean?" I asked warily.

"Potatoes are like people. They're all basically the same, but they do have subtle differences that create havoc and disarray if they're left on their own. You see it in regular potato chips the way they're all dissimilar," he explained with distaste. "But if you mash them all into a uniform paste, you can stamp them out into identical forms; bake them; and bring unity, order, and perfection."

My eyes widened in alarm as the Red Menace completed his analogy.

"I intend to do the same thing with the people of Superopolis, and Pseudo-Chips will be my tool for accomplishing it."

CHAPTER ELEVEN

Promises, Promises

The Red Menace had admitted right to our faces that he was using the chips as his tool to complete his life-long plot against the people of Superopolis. And yet I still had no idea what exactly he was trying to pull off, let alone how he intended to use the chips to do it. The best thing to do would be to stop people from eating them. But how?

As I arrived at school on Thursday, another problem reared its ugly head—so to speak. Melonhead was standing next to the school flagpole attempting to give a speech.

"Attenthun, fellow thtudenth of Watthon Elementary," he was spitting and spattering. "Choothe me ath your clath prethident and I promithe that I'll bring AI himthelf to the thchool to therve uth hith Amathing Theudo-Chipth during every thingle clath."

Melonhead's ability to deliver on such a promise was impossible—but as with any good politician, he didn't let that stop him. Fortunately no one was hearing his pandering pledges. There was too much competition for my schoolmates' attention.

Plasma Girl and Little Miss Bubbles were handing out miniature tea scones that they had spent all last night baking in their Amazing Indestructo Thermal Ovens. They were passing them out to anyone who would come close enough to hear Tadpole making his own speech. The Spore was trying something similar as part of his unchallenged race to be class coroner, but so much mold had spread over the cookies he was giving out that he wasn't getting any takers. That didn't seem to bother him, though, and he stopped his speech every few minutes to eat another one himself.

Transparent Girl hadn't let up at all in her campaign against me for treasurer. She wasn't even attempting to be subtle. She had gone straight to handing out money. But despite her offer of a dime to anyone who would come close enough to hear Melonhead speak, she still wasn't succeeding in drawing a crowd to him.

"No one wants to stop and listen," she complained to Cannonball, who had also noticed the difficulty his candidate was having in attracting any attention.

"Hmm. Give me a hand," he said to his best friend, Lobster Boy, who was standing next to him. But Lobster

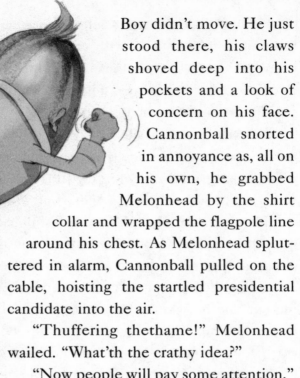

Boy didn't move. He just stood there, his claws shoved deep into his pockets and a look of concern on his face. Cannonball snorted in annoyance as, all on his own, he grabbed Melonhead by the shirt collar and wrapped the flagpole line around his chest. As Melonhead spluttered in alarm, Cannonball pulled on the cable, hoisting the startled presidential candidate into the air.

"Thuffering thethame!" Melonhead wailed. "What'th the crathy idea?"

"Now people will pay some attention," Cannonball declared confidently.

Sure enough, kids came wandering from all directions, not wanting to miss the physical humiliation of one of their fellow students.

"There. You've got a crowd," the bully told him. "So talk—and remember what I told you to say."

"Yeth, thir," replied a clearly

intimidated Melonhead. "If elected, fellow thtudenth, I promithe that everyone will rethieve thtraight Ath on their report cardth, no matter how bad their gradeth are. I will altho abolith all tethting and quiththeth."

The crowd erupted in an approving cheer despite the ridiculous impossibility of what Melonhead was promising.

Tadpole was completely peeved by this new ploy, and I watched as he whispered something in Stench's ear. It was imperative that this speech be broken up before Melonhead made any more preposterous pledges. As Stench elbowed his way to the center of the crowd around the flagpole, I knew what solution Tadpole had proposed. I held my breath and backed away quickly. A moment later a loud noise ripped through the mob of kids, and there was a mass stampede outward from the center amid shrieks and cries of horror. A space instantly cleared to reveal a totally embarrassed-looking Stench. I felt bad for him as he removed a spray can from his utility belt and began to deodorize the air around him. At least he had broken up the crowd.

Following the mob into the school, we all tried to reassure Stench.

"Don't be embarrassed." Plasma Girl patted him on the back. "That was the fastest way to deal with the situation, and you did it perfectly."

"Except he won't be able to be there every time Cannonball tries spreading his garbage around," Tadpole complained. "I say we just start making even bigger promises."

"But that isn't right," protested Plasma Girl. "We can't sink to their level."

"Why not?" Tadpole complained. "What's the point of losing honorably?"

"Plasma Girl's right," I agreed. "Their lies will eventually get them in trouble."

Tadpole looked skeptical, but the first bell of the day rang before he could respond. As we turned to head for the front doors, a voice overhead squeaked miserably.

"Thay, I don't thuppothe thomeone would mind helping me down?"

Lobster Boy stopped for a moment as if he was going to assist Melonhead, but then he kept walking, never removing his claws from his pockets.

The thought of leaving Melonhead hanging was tempting, but in the end, Stench and I helped lower him to the ground. He didn't even bother to thank us.

Inside the classroom, the campaigning continued. Cannonball was announcing to the class that if he and Melonhead were elected, everyone in the class would be made a member of the League of Ultimate Goodness.

It's true that Cannonball's uncle, the Crimson Creampuff, was in the league, but I doubted he had that kind of pull. Nevertheless, my classmates were falling for it.

Tadpole sat at his desk fuming as he watched any hope of victory being stolen out from under him. Plasma Girl was doing her best to calm down her running mate.

"We can't win by copying their tactics," she said. "We need an original strategy of our own."

"I'll show you an original strategy," he growled. Without even turning around, Tadpole's tongue shot out and looped behind him to where Cannonball stood atop his desk speaking. His tongue wrapped around the leg of the desk and gave it a sharp tug.

In mid-sentence, Cannonball came tumbling down, sending all my classmates running. It was pure mayhem as Miss Marble entered the room. She didn't even bother to say anything before she turned us all into living statues. I was caught in an uncomfortable twist of my waist, having been in the process of turning to witness Cannonball's downfall. But it was nothing compared to Cannonball himself. Flat on his back, both his legs and arms were stretched up toward the ceiling, like a turtle stuck on its back. The most hysterical bug-eyed scream I had ever seen was frozen on his face. I would have laughed if I could have.

"You're worse than a pack of wild animals," Miss

Marble began to rant, "which makes today's activity all the more appropriate. Rather than wasting time teaching you things you'll forget an hour later, today we're going on a field trip."

A class trip! A chance to get out of the school for the day and investigate some (usually boring—but who cares?) part of Superopolis! I hoped it would be someplace fun.

"This trip is to see something I know you'll all *love*," Miss Marble continued with sarcasm. She smirked, and then went in for the kill.

"Today you'll have the pleasure of hearing a live political speech from none other than Mayor Whitewash himself."

As her power began to wear off, I heard the first groans issuing from the mouths of my classmates. Yet even as my own range of movement returned, I noticed that her triumphant grin was fading. There was more that she hadn't told us.

"Of course," she added with a reluctant sigh, "the speech will be taking place at the Superopolis Zoo."

The class erupted in cheers, as Miss Marble rolled her eyes in annoyance.

CHAPTER TWELVE

What's New at the Zoo?

The school bus dropped us off at the main entrance to the Superopolis Zoo. It was a beautiful, mild October day and the place was busier than normal. There were a number of school field trips just like ours, and even a few people—very few—who had come specifically to hear the mayor's speech.

Mayor Whitewash had always been a successful politician because of his power to convince people to agree with whatever he said. It wasn't as powerful a gift as the Red Menace's ability to make people *do* whatever he said, but I wondered if he couldn't still somehow convince people to stop eating Pseudo-Chips. I was hoping this unexpected trip to the zoo might provide an opportunity for me to enlist his help.

Miss Marble led us through the twisting trails of

THE SUPEROPOLIS ZOO

With animals of almost every known species, the Superopolis Zoo provides a serene setting for the city's wildlife. It also keeps them safe from a city of superpowered humans, who are often the most dangerous animals around. How the zoo was populated, given its location in an environment devoid of any natural fauna, is a mystery of little interest to anyone.

the zoo, past cages of lions and swamps full of alligators, fields of elephants and pools of penguins, hills riddled with prairie dogs and trees full of monkeys. I had been here dozens of times, but today something seemed odd.

Usually the animals went about their business oblivious to the humans strolling around looking at them. Yet today I had the distinct impression that *they* were watching *us*. The first thing I noticed was a group of six tropical birds perched atop a chain-link fence looking right at us. Sparkplug noticed them, too, and, being a creep, reached over to touch the fence. A jolt of electricity coursed through the metal fence, and the shocked birds scattered amid squawks of alarm.

The seal pool was coming up next on our right, and Cannonball ran up to the edge, with Lobster Boy close behind him, his claws still shoved in his pockets. The fat jerk was oblivious of the seal staring at him in a very unseal-like manner.

"I've got seafood," he said, coaxing the seal to come forward as he kept his hands behind his back like he was holding a fish. "Come and get the seafood."

"Cannonball," Lobster Boy said as they watched the seal crawling forward, "you don't have any seafood."

"Don't I?" He smirked as he grabbed Lobster Boy and hoisted him into the air above the seal pool.

"HELP!" Lobster Boy's claws finally came out of his pockets and they began to clench and unclench in panic as Cannonball held him by his feet over the pool. The seal didn't appear the least bit pleased and honked in annoyance.

"What's wrong with lobster?" Cannonball laughed as he set his "friend" back onto the ground. Lobster Boy quickly shoved his claws back into his pockets, but not before I noticed that they weren't their usual bright red. In fact, they were nearly flesh colored.

Those of us who had witnessed this odd incident now hurried to catch up with the rest of our classmates who were huddled around the monkey cages. The monkeys were all getting riled by peanuts that were being pelted at them seemingly from nowhere. I didn't even need to hear her nasty laugh to know that Transparent Girl was the one mistreating them. Fortunately, Miss Marble noticed as well and moved the group quickly along.

"Are you guys noticing how strangely the animals are behaving?" I whispered to my teammates.

"There's definitely something odd about these aardvarks," Tadpole said as we passed their pen. The two aardvarks were fascinated by Tadpole's tongue as he stuck it out at them. They responded by sticking their tongues out at him.

We made our way to the center of the zoo, where Miss Marble brought us to a stop in front of a stage that had been set up. A large crowd had gathered, but it soon became clear that most of the people assembled were there to see the zoo's newest and most popular exhibit just across from the stage. It was an attraction that I was in many ways responsible for.

Safely behind mighty steel bars was a genuine, live velociraptor. A week earlier, he had been living the normal life of a dinosaur sixty-five million years ago. But when Superopolis took that wild ride into the past—and then back to the present—the dinosaur came along with us. It was quickly decided it should be placed in the zoo, since it just wouldn't have been wise to let a velociraptor roam about the city on its own.

My classmates immediately wandered toward the cage, even though Mayor Whitewash was up on the dais waiting to give his speech. Irritated that an exhibit was grabbing all the attention away from him, he turned to his wife standing with him.

"Blanche, go take care of that distraction."

The woman turned white as a sheet then hurried off the stage. Thanks to her size she had no problem positioning herself in such a way that she completely blocked the view of the dinosaur cage. Reluctantly the crowd turned its attention back to the mayor.

"Welcome, Superopolitans young and old," the mayor began. That was as far as he got before being interrupted by one of the "old" Superopolitans in the audience.

"What are you going to do to help those of us on fixed incomes afford the increasing price of potato chips? These newfangled chips are so consarned delicious we can't resist them. But they cost a whopping ten cents a can more than Dr. Telomere's did."

A bunch of other old people began seconding his complaint.

"Of course, of course," the mayor said reassuringly. "I always take the concerns of our elderly citizens seriously, seeing as how they're often the only ones who vote."

He glanced nervously at his wife, who shrugged her shoulders as she once again drained of color. That was all the time he needed to come up with a plan.

"That's exactly why I'm proposing that the city purchase every empty canister of the Amazing Indestructo's Amazing Pseudo-Chips for a dime. Not only can you make back the extra ten cents the chips cost, but you can also gather up the canisters that others are too lazy to redeem and make even more money to fund your retirements. I think you can all agree with that idea."

He made that announcement with the sureness of a man who had never had anyone disagree with him.

Until now.

The old people in the crowd erupted in jeers.

"But that would require effort on our part," one woman complained.

"Yeah," added another. "Why can't there just be a

government grant that gives us the money as if we *had* redeemed the cans without us actually having to do the work?"

The mayor looked shocked. No one had ever questioned one of his statements or proposals. I was shocked, too. My idea for enlisting his aid to steer people away from Pseudo-Chips was collapsing in front of me. What had happened to the mayor's power?

"Mithter Mayor?" I turned around in surprise to see Melonhead eagerly raising his hand. "Thurely you mutht know that the prithe of Amathing Indethtructo comic bookth have rithen by twenty-five thenth in jutht the latht year. Wouldn't thuch a program be perfect for that crithith?"

"Of course not, son," the mayor replied as he tried to shake off his panic over his failure with his older constituents. "You're not old enough to vote. And even when you are old enough, statistics show that you probably won't bother. But old people *do* vote, and could very well vote me out of office." I looked at the various old people in the crowd, all of whom looked ready to prove the mayor right. "That's why I pander to their every whim and why I'm proud to announce my new Pseudo-Chip Senior Citizen Rebate Grant Program."

The old people all let out a cheer.

"But you're running unopposed," I shouted out.

"That isn't completely true," the mayor corrected me. "There may not be another candidate on the ballot, but I'm not the only choice. I live in constant fear that 'none of the above' could someday be elected mayor."

The saddest thing was that he could be so honest about his motivations without causing any outrage. Or so I thought.

"Perhaps your greatest concern, Mayor, should be whether you're elected to be someone else's meal."

All heads turned toward the mayor's wife, which was the direction from which the eerie voice had come.

"Blanche . . . ?" the mayor started to say.

She was whiter than anyone had ever seen her before and had a look of sheer terror on her face. She quickly darted back to her husband on the stage, and we could all once again view the zoo's latest attraction.

"Excellent," the dinosaur spoke again. "I see I have your full and undivided attention."

CHAPTER THIRTEEN

Zoo Hullabaloo

Just then, chaos erupted throughout the zoo. Every animal in every cage suddenly began bursting its barriers. To describe what happened next as hysteria would be a massive understatement. It was pandamonium, it was otter chaos, it was an albatross-ity, it was . . . well . . . it was a whole bunch of other really bad animal puns.

There was nothing strange about seeing a person in Superopolis doing something unusual. But animals behaving bizarrely was a whole different story. People always had superpowers. Animals did not. Until now.

Some of them instantly went for payback. The birds that Sparkplug had shocked off their perch came dive-bombing right toward him. At the last possible moment they pulled back up, but not before pelting him with droppings.

"Eewwww!" my classmates and I exclaimed simultaneously.

But it was worse than just getting splattered with bird poop, if you can imagine such a thing. What these birds had left behind stuck to Sparkplug like glue, and the more he struggled, the more he found himself being coated with the stinky, sticky mess.

Not everyone was sympathetic. Cannonball was laughing his butt off, though he should have been paying more attention to his own safety. The seal he had humiliated just moments earlier had quietly sidled up behind him. Still laughing hysterically, Cannonball turned around, only to go silent as he noticed the seal glaring at him. Before he could react, the seal reared up and gave his front flippers one solid clap creating a massive shock wave that sent Cannonball rolling more than a hundred feet away.

"These animals have developed some remarkable abilities, wouldn't you say?"

I turned to the dinosaur inside the cage. He was speaking directly to me.

"As have I," he continued. "You may call me Gore."

"Gore?" I repeated, baffled by the impossibility of what I was hearing. "But how did you . . . ?"

"I'm really not certain," he replied. "I woke up in this cage the other morning with the remarkable ability to not only understand the languages of all creatures but also to speak them."

"Including humans," I added numbly.

"Yes." Gore nodded. "Well, you are just animals yourselves, despite your delusions to the contrary. Your language is, however, quite sophisticated—though not as highly developed as that of the orangutan or the chipmunk."

"Chipmunks speak?" I asked, momentarily distracted from the mayhem around me.

"All creatures have ways to communicate with each other." Gore broke into a pleased grin revealing rows of impossibly sharp teeth. "And language, of course, is the key to knowledge. For instance, thanks to the newspapers that line my cage I've come to fully understand where I am and how I got here. That's how I also happen to know that you, young human, are responsible for me being brought here to this time. I recognized you from your photo."

"But I have no way of sending you back," I said, assuming that was his ultimate goal.

"Oh, I have no desire to go back," he replied almost cheerily. "I realize that everything I knew of my past was destroyed just moments after you brought me forward to this time. That enormous meteor was coming—with or without you being there—along with the complete extinction of my race. There is nothing for me to go back to even if I could."

"Then what are you after?" I asked.

"I'm fascinated by this time and its contradictions—incredible technology, yet simpleminded individuals; people with amazing powers, but who use them in meaningless ways. Can these animals utilize their new abilities in any poorer a manner? Perhaps. Perhaps not. I'm fascinated to see. I'm also incredibly curious as to how these powers came about."

Where *did* these animals' powers come from? Then I did a double take. Where did *anyone's* power come from? The dinosaur had planted a question in my brain that crowded out all other thoughts. Maybe people *haven't* always had superabilities. What if there *is* something that causes powers to develop?

"Believe me, *I* won't waste this gift that has befallen me," Gore concluded, snapping me back to the situation at hand. "I merely wanted to thank you for having made it possible."

I was too surprised to even respond. Then he made some high-pitched clucking noises and small whirling dervishes plunged into the crowd. They were only about two feet tall, but they caused a panic that sent everyone fleeing. One of them stopped long enough for me to see that they were penguins.

My friends and I were about to run from the wildly spinning critters when we heard a strange whirring sound above us. I looked up to see a whole mess of monkeys hovering in the air, their tails spinning madly above them like helicopter blades. They began pelting the stampeding crowd with nuts, and my teammates and I backed against the cage to avoid being hit.

If we had run off like most of the crowd, we would have missed it when one of the monkeys landed, depositing an enormous king cobra onto the pavement in front of the dinosaur exhibit. The snake slithered up to the front of the cage as the velociraptor watched approvingly. Rising to its full height, the cobra reared back and spit a huge wad of something onto the bars of the enclosure. Within seconds they began to bubble, smoke, and hiss as a powerful acid ate through three or four of the steel bars.

"Thank you, my friends," the dinosaur said to the animals as he knocked aside what little remained of his barrier and stepped out onto the pavement in front of us.

"As the only one among these creatures who can understand all their languages, I seem to have become their de facto leader," he informed us. "Now what do you suppose happened to *your* leader? He and I really need to speak."

We looked up at the stage, but the mayor and his wife had already hit the trail running. Despite our fear, my teammates and I held our ground.

"Children, please do as your friends have done and run away," Gore said calmly. "I have no intention of harming you, but please don't block my path. I must find your mayor."

"You claim to understand everything," I said, "but clearly you don't understand what it means to be a hero."

"Logic dictates that one does only what is in one's own best interests," Gore lectured. "Yet your species has a remarkable tendency to do things that provide no apparent advantage. Most prove detrimental. Yet I

concede that occasionally these heroic actions deliver benefits that could not have been calculated in advance."

"All risk. No reward," said Stench as he picked up one of the iron bars and bent it in half. "Bring it on."

"Very well." The velociraptor sighed. "That meteor from which you rescued me destroyed my species and everything with which I was familiar. Yet, ironically, it also brought me great riches. Without it I would not have become the enlightened creature that now stands before you. Part of enlightenment includes knowing when it is best to avoid a confrontation not fully in one's favor."

The dinosaur made an intense growling noise and a leopard bolted up beside him. To our complete amazement, the leopard removed one of its spots, stretched it to the size of a manhole, and tossed it onto the ground. Before we even had a chance to react, the velociraptor jumped onto, and then *into*, the spot, vanishing from sight.

CHAPTER FOURTEEN

Cause...

The papers on Friday morning were jammed full of stories about the sudden rampage of newly powerful zoo animals. *The Hero Herald*'s headline used a pun I had missed, screaming: BAD GNUS AT THE ZOO!! *The Superopolis Times* was a little more sedate and a lot more alliterative with: POWER PETS PUZZLE POPULACE, despite the fact that the animals in question were hardly "pets." Neither paper mentioned the mysterious failure of Mayor Whitewash's power. Or maybe they just missed it amid the general chaos.

As usual, *The Weekly Daily* was just catching up to the events involving Professor Brain-Drain's attempt to transport Superopolis back in time to be destroyed. They even had a photo of the approaching meteor. It was the first chance I'd had to look at it closely. I wondered what it was made of. There was something familiar about it, but I couldn't put my finger on what. Gore's comment that the meteor had brought him great riches still echoed in my brain.

"Say, this could be a perfect opportunity for the New New Crusaders," my dad said between gulps of orange juice and handfuls of Eggs 'n' Bacon flavored Pseudo-Chips. He still hadn't revealed to my mother that his team had been fired as the Maximizer Brand spokesteam. "Dumb animals wouldn't stand a chance against the NNC."

"I wouldn't assume they're so dumb," I said as I set down the paper and poured myself a bowl of sugar-flavored Power Pellets. "That dinosaur I talked with sounded more intelligent than most people."

"And just where did their powers come from?" asked my mom as she handed me an extrachilled pitcher of milk for my cereal.

"That's exactly what I'm wondering," I responded, though I was really wondering: Where does *anyone's* power come from?

If I could solve the mystery of how animals that never had powers before now did, it could help me answer the biggest question of my life. After all, if animals could suddenly develop superpowers, then *why not me?*

All the way to school, I became more and more excited at the possibilities. By the time I got there, I was in a great mood. The same could not be said for my classmates. Each one of them seemed to be in various states of depression, ranging from mild in the case of the Spore (who always seemed a little morose) and Somnia (who dozed fitfully as a trail of drool ran from her mouth) to extreme in the case of Lobster Boy who was so slumped in his chair that his chin rested on his desk. My teammates were acting down as well.

"Yesterday was so unsettling." Plasma Girl sighed. "And the thought that those animals are still out there kept me awake half the night."

"Me, too," Stench agreed. "I had an opportunity to embarrass my brother, Fuzz, this morning, but I just didn't feel up to it."

"What happened?" Tadpole asked with only a slight degree of curiosity.

"I caught him in the bathroom growing hair under his arms while he talked to his reflection in the mirror about how impressed all the "chicks" would be. All I had to do was throw open the door. My mom was standing in the hall and would have seen it instantly."

"He didn't really say 'chicks,' did he?" Plasma Girl said with annoyance. "That is so demeaning to women."

"He didn't mean baby chickens?" I caught Hal mumble, mildly perplexed.

"That's Fuzz," Stench said in a way that carried with it a lifetime of irritation with his older brother.

Just then Miss Marble came into the room. She didn't seem herself either—she was actually in a good mood.

"Well, I'm glad to see we all managed to survive our day at the zoo," she said as she counted heads. "I have no idea what happened yesterday, but I hope 'animals with superpowers' is a situation that will go away just as quickly as it appeared."

"Where can their powers have come from?" asked Transparent Girl.

"Clearly this was the work of some previously unknown supervillain whose own power is the ability to bestow powers on animals," said Miss Marble.

This seemed like a bit of a stretch to me.

"Maybe whatever causes people to have powers has also now affected these animals," I piped in.

Everyone in the class looked at me as if I had said something inexcusable. Silent shock hung in the air until . . .

"What do you mean *causes* people to have powers?"

The Quake rumbled from the back of the room. I turned to see that she had raised her fist menacingly at me.

"Yeah, people just *have* powers," Cannonball added. "Except you, anyway!"

The nastier kids laughed as my face flushed red. My own friends didn't laugh, but I could tell they were embarrassed by what I had said.

"Everyone knows that a superpower is what makes someone unique and special," said Little Miss Bubbles. "It's only natural." She giggled amid an eruption of bubbles.

"But what if it's not?" I pressed, despite the discomfort of my friends. "What if something causes it? And now that same thing has affected these animals."

"Miss Marble," wailed Puddle Boy as a pool of liquid rapidly spread out from under his desk, "Ordinary Boy says there's nothing special about my power!"

"He has to say that," a voice came from the cloud that encased Foggybottom, "because there's nothing special about *him*."

I felt humiliated as most of the class laughed. My attempt at asking a legitimate question was only drawing scorn.

"Don't let O Boy put us down, Miss Marble," demanded Transparent Girl. "And we have to make certain he isn't elected to a post as important as class treasurer."

"I'm not trying to put anyone down," I insisted. "I'm just trying to get answers. Isn't the whole point of school to seek out knowledge?"

"Not particularly," Miss Marble responded gloomily. "I'm afraid the point of school isn't so much about learning things as it is learning not to say things that irritate other people."

"But how else do we gain knowledge?" I asked. "Shouldn't we always be asking questions and trying to use what we discover to make life better?"

"You're free to do all that"—Miss Marble nodded—"as long as you don't upset anyone in the process or challenge any of their beliefs."

"In a democrathy, the majority dethideth what'th right," Melonhead splattered. "Ithn't that tho, Mith Marble?"

"Sadly, you appear to be correct." She sighed as the final shred of her good mood evaporated.

"But what if they're wrong?" I added meekly, already feeling beaten.

"Tho let'th thettle thith the democratic way by cathting voteth," Melonhead proposed. "Whoever thinkth our powerth are an intheperable part of who we are, raithe your hand!"

I didn't even need to look to know that every hand had shot up. The only stab of pain came as I realized that all my teammates had raised theirs as well. But then I got a shock. In the back row I saw that Lobster Boy had kept his hand down. In fact he still had both of his claws shoved in his lap. His head was no longer slumped on his desk, though. Now it was raised in alarm. Cannonball noticed the same time I did.

"Put your hand up, shell brain," he threatened as he grabbed Lobster Boy's arm and forced it into the air.

It was pretty hard to miss the oven mitt that he was wearing over his claw. Cannonball was taken aback by it at first, too, but then, with a nasty sneer on his face, he yanked off the big poofy glove to reveal a perfectly ordinary, absolutely human . . . hand.

NAME: Lobster Boy. **POWER:** Two fully manipulable pinchers in place of hands. **LIMITATIONS:** He'll never play the piano well. **CAREER:** A deathly fear of drawn butter rules out any future in the restaurant business. **CLASSIFICATION:** May just claw his way to the top yet.

CHAPTER FIFTEEN

. . . and Effects

My own questions about the origin of power were quickly overshadowed by the shock surrounding the transformation of Lobster Boy into . . . well . . . Hand Boy. But as Miss Marble hustled Lobster Boy off to the school nurse and sent the rest of us out for an early recess, my friends caught up to me.

"What were you thinking?" Tadpole asked as we followed our classmates from the room. "Are you determined to enrage every kid in our class with that where-do-powers-come-from bit?"

"For a while there I thought we were going to have to rescue you," Stench added.

"Yeah," agreed Plasma Girl, "what *was* all that stuff you were talking about?"

"My power is . . . well . . . my power," Halogen Boy said in almost a whisper as he struggled to verbalize his feelings.

By this time, I realized how upset people could get over the mere suggestion that something so key to their identity might actually just be a side effect of something else.

"Hal," I responded as we paused in the hallway, "you're special because of who you are. Your power is just one aspect out of millions that make you the unique person that you are."

"But it's the most important—" Tadpole started to say before catching himself. He glanced at me guiltily.

"Look, no one knows better than I do what it's like having no power."

"Lobster Boy is going to get a chance to find out," Tadpole said in a way I think he meant to sound supportive but didn't.

"Yeah," asked Stench, "what could have caused such an effect?"

"Exactly!" I said as I seized on what he had said. "Cause and effect. Nothing happens without *something* causing it to happen."

"What do you mean?" Plasma Girl questioned me suspiciously.

"Take flowers for instance," I replied. "No one would say they're not special. But they exist because the rain falls and the sun shines on them. Take either away, and you'd have no flowers."

I could tell by the expressions on their faces that they were beginning to get my point.

"Or just look at the ocean's tides," I said. "The waves look like they're just happening on their own, but they're really not. The gravity of the moon is tugging at the sea and causing the waves to wash back and forth. Without the moon, the ocean would sit practically still."

"I think I see what you mean." Plasma Girl nodded.

"Something causes everything! Your power is no different," I added, coming back to my original point. "That doesn't mean that it's not incredibly special and important to who you are."

"I guess that's true," Halogen Boy agreed as he brightened considerably.

"And even without a power, you're pretty special, too," Plasma Girl said as she placed a hand on my shoulder.

I blushed beet red, just as Tadpole and Stench's howling laughter echoed through the empty hallway.

"You *are* special, O Boy!" Tadpole mocked in a bad imitation of Plasma Girl as even Hal joined in the laughter.

"Shut up," Plasma Girl said as she punched Tadpole in the arm.

That just set them laughing harder, and I slumped my shoulders in embarrassment.

"What is *wrong* with boys, anyway?" she huffed as she stalked ahead of us and pushed open the school's front door. My friends' laughter quickly faded as we noticed the rest of our classmates standing outside as still as statues. At first I thought Miss Marble had returned and used her power on them. Then I noticed what had them so transfixed.

"Oh, my gosh!" Plasma Girl exclaimed. "What is going on out here?!"

There were animals everywhere. There were grizzlies slashing our school bus's tires; snakes slithering up the flagpole; and, yes, even monkeys on the monkey bars. At first I thought they were fighting with each other. But then I realized they were actually locked in battle with—

"It's the League of Ultimate Goodness!" Tadpole blurted out in amazement.

It was true! The entire league was spread out across our school yard, engaged in a titanic struggle with hordes of zoo creatures.

"These animals ambushed us," the Crimson Creampuff hollered as he came running straight for us. "Get to safety, kids!"

Apparently he was trying to follow his own advice. But before he could find a place to hide, a rhinoceros that was barreling after him hoisted him into the air and began spinning the spongy superhero on the tip of

his horn like a giant basketball.

There were LUGs everywhere, but they seemed to be exceeding even *their* high standards of incompetence. Featherweight was drifting back and forth between two playful mountain lions, who were intrigued by his feathery, birdlike costume. Moleman was buried in the ground to his waist while a family of squirrels used their tails like slingshots to pelt him with nuts. And then I spotted Cap'n Blowhole, who was facing off against a polar bear.

"Arrrgghh, matey!" he gloated as a plume of water shot out of his head, "we'll be seein' if yer any match fer the cap'n."

The polar bear answered the challenge by rearing up on his hind legs and letting out a freezing blast of breath. Cap'n Blowhole's water spout froze solid instantly.

"Sh-sh-sh-shiver me timbers," he cried in alarm as the suddenly top-heavy weight of his ice plume tipped him over headfirst.

In the midst of the fracas, a figure descended from the sky, shouting advice to the bewildered group of heroes. It was the Amazing Indestructo.

As he cut the power on his jet pack, I assumed he was going to join the battle against the zoo animals. Instead, he moved over to relative safety near me and my classmates.

"Look, it's AI!" the Banshee screamed in a way that no one could miss, including AI himself.

"Sheeesh!" he said with a cringe as he covered his ears. "Can't you see I'm trying to oversee this important battle?"

"Maybe you should actually be out there helping for a change," I said as I stepped up alongside him.

The Amazing Indestructo's eyes narrowed in annoyance as he turned and saw me.

"Oh, it's you." He sniffed dismissively. "Maybe you should just step back with the rest of the children where you won't be in the way."

"But the safest spot in any battle is usually right next to you," I countered.

"Suit yourself," he said as his face flushed red. "I have to concentrate on bringing this scourge of super-powered animals to an end."

As he returned to doing nothing, I focused on the battle before us. Spaghetti Man was shooting strands of pasta from his fingertips in an attempt to immobilize the spindly legs of a giraffe. Of course the giraffe broke through them instantly and then proceeded to stretch its neck a good twenty feet, wrapping it around Spaghetti Man like a boa constrictor.

"Hellllp!!" he cried. "This-a giraffe . . . her neck is like-a linguini!"

NAME: Spaghetti Man. **POWER:** An ability to fire strands of wet spaghetti from his fingertips. **LIMITATIONS:** The sauce has to be prepared the traditional way. **CAREER:** Despite the obvious career one would have expected, given his family's pasta business, Spaghetti Man turned to a life of crime fighting, eventually joining the League of Ultimate Goodness. **CLASSIFICATION:** As dangerous to criminals as a wet noodle.

"I see the league is performing at their usual level of efficiency," I commented to the Amazing Indestructo.

"Just give 'em a chance . . ." he started to say, and then fell silent.

I followed his eyes to where they had focused on an elephant across the playground. It had just begun to charge toward us.

"Uh-oh," I agreed, as at the exact same moment the school bell rang and kids from all the other classes came rushing out for the morning recess. "You've got to do something."

"Are you kidding?" AI blurted out. "Look at the size of that thing. I'm getting out of here."

"You're indestructible!" I screamed back at him. "Act like it for a change."

He was about to start up his jet pack, but I reached over and yanked out one of its power cables.

"Hey!" he yelled. "What are you trying to do?"

"You're not going to run out on your fans, are you? It's going to really hurt your sales if anything happens to a group of kids while you stand by," I pointed out as both he and I noticed the rampaging elephant getting closer and closer.

The Human Compass was right in its path but then darted off to the north. Major Bummer, who sat nearby with his head slumped while a pack of hyenas ridiculed him, simply got up and walked in the opposite direction. Whistlin' Dixie managed to get her lasso around one of the elephant's tusks, but she was no match for an animal that size, and her rope was yanked right out of her hands. That left only the Amazing Indestructo, who, realizing he had no choice, decided to make the most of the situation.

"Step back kids," he boomed in his best TV hero voice. "The Amazing Indestructo is here to save the day."

As the kids let out a cheer, he barreled straight at the charging beast. It didn't take long for AI to notice with horror that the elephant had suddenly sprouted a second set of tusks. And then a third. And then a fourth, fifth, and sixth. I could only imagine the horror in the Amazing Indestructo's eyes. But it was too late for him to do anything now.

Like the thundering sound of a dozen cannons, the indestructible hero and the unstoppable force collided. When the dust finally cleared, none of us could believe what we saw. The multitusked elephant had been knocked back on its rear and looked a little dazed. But crumpled in a heap in front of him was the Amazing Indestructo. He was practically pulverized.

"Ow . . ." was the one solitary word that emerged softly from his contorted lips.

We all held our collective breath as Whistlin' Dixie ran to his aid.

"Tarnation! Someone git some help," she hollered in a panic. "The Amazing Indestructo's been—" the very impossibility of the word caught in her voice "—hurt!"

CHAPTER SIXTEEN

Faded Genes

It wasn't hard to guess what was going to be on the front page of the newspaper on Saturday morning. I retrieved our copy of the *Superopolis Times* from the front porch and there, front and center, was one of the largest headlines I'd ever seen: AI INJURED!!!! And yes, it had four exclamation points. Below, in slightly smaller type, it asked the question: INDESTRUCTIBLE NO MORE?? Here they used only two question marks. I brought it into the kitchen where Mom and Dad were preparing breakfast.

"I can't believe it," my dad said as he read the head-line over my shoulder. "How could someone who's indestructible be hurt by anything?"

Dad had a frying pan resting on his palm and was busy scrambling eggs. My mom was setting out milk, orange juice, and a bowl of AI's Maple Glazed Pseudo-Chips. I sampled one of them. It was as disgusting as you might imagine.

"If he were still around, I might think that Professor Brain-Drain was somehow responsible for this," Mom said as she focused her gaze on my glass of milk to get it extra cold. "But clearly he isn't."

"Thanks to our little hero," my dad said proudly as he gave me a mock punch in the arm.

Instinctively, I recoiled. Not because Dad had hit me too hard, but rather to keep from getting an imprint of his superhot hand on my skin. Oddly, his fist was only lukewarm at best. I probably wouldn't have thought anything more about it, except Dad brought over the frying pan and proceeded to scrape a portion of half-cooked, curdled-looking eggs onto my plate.

"Dad, are you okay?" I asked. My mom was suddenly concerned as well.

"Thermo, what's the matter?"

"Nothing is wrong," he replied, obviously agitated. "Everything is just fine."

For about thirty seconds he succeeded in maintaining his facade of confidence—then he broke down and began blubbering into his hands.

"I don't know what's happening," he sobbed as only a mild hint of steam was given off. "Ever since I woke up, I haven't been able to generate anything other than a mild heat. What's happening to me?! Oh, and we also got fired as the spokesteam for Maximizer Brand Snack Cakes."

"There, there, dear," she attempted to calm him. "Everything will be— Wait, you also got fired?"

I nodded encouragingly to my dad to fess up as I picked up my glass of milk. I hadn't taken more than a sip before my blood ran cold—for the simple reason that my milk was anything *but* cold.

"Mom?" I asked nervously as I set the glass back down. "How are you feeling?"

"I'm just fine," she snapped back a little peevishly. "See?"

She took a hard stare at my orange juice, I think in an attempt to freeze it solid. But nothing happened. In desperation, she tried again—and failed again. Her face betrayed a number of emotions all at once—fear, frustration, worry—and then her natural calm took control.

"Whatever has affected the Amazing Indestructo is clearly affecting us as well," she admitted. "With or without powers, it's up to us to figure out the cause."

The cause! Of course! Something had to be causing this loss of power that had hit Mayor Whitewash, Lobster Boy, AI, and now my parents. What had changed over the last week that could possibly be behind this? Then I looked at the bowl of chips, and the Red Menace's threat came back to me. He had said he was going to make everybody equal. Taking away their powers would certainly accomplish that, but could his Pseudo-Chips really do that?

"Mom, Dad! Maybe it's the chips!" I blurted out.

"What do you mean, OB?" my mom asked.

"Well," I said. "They *are* the only thing that's changed in our day-to-day routine. Maybe they're responsible for your power loss!"

"That's ridiculous," my mom said defensively. "How could potato chips do something like that?"

"I don't know," I admitted, "but nothing else makes sense. I think you should stop eating them."

"Don't be silly." My mom laughed. "Just because you don't like them is no reason to scare us away from them."

"I can't lose my power *and* my Pseudo-Chips in the same day," my dad said, sniffling. "I just couldn't handle it."

"You won't need to, dear," my mom said confidently as she stood up. "We're going to figure out the real cause of this mystery. It's time to gather up the New—" she paused only momentarily, and with only a hint of a cringe "—New Crusaders."

"It'll be just like old times," Dad said with a wide grin. "Thermo and Snowflake, together again on the job."

While my parents planned their new mission, I remained at the table, my own concern undiminished. My parents were still under the control of the Red Menace, so I was going to have to find someone who wasn't. I was going to need the Junior Leaguers.

I called everyone to announce an unscheduled emergency meeting and then practically ran to Stench's house. I was in such a hurry that I didn't even notice the wire that had been pulled tight between two particularly close piles of tires in his dad's junkyard. I fell right into Fuzz Boy's trap. Zippy appeared out of nowhere, grabbed my legs, and pinned them to the ground. Fuzz Boy was on me a second later, pulling back each of my arms and kneeling on them, leaving me totally immobile.

"We set this trap to catch some of these freaky animals," Fuzz Boy sneered. "But you'll do fine instead."

"Do something really funny, Fuzz," Zippy said with a crazy grin on his face, "like growing hair in his ears."

"I think what O Boy here is going to need when I'm done with him is an all-over shave," Fuzz Boy said menacingly. "And we'll start with a *really* long beard."

As much as I struggled, I was no match for the two fourteen-year-olds, and Fuzz Boy cupped his hands around my cheeks and chin. I felt a tickle as the beard began to grow, but then I sensed some irritation on Fuzz Boy's part.

"What's the matter?" Zippy asked. "That's not much of a beard."

"Give me a second," Fuzz Boy said in obvious annoyance. "I'm working on it."

But nothing more was growing, with the exception of Fuzz Boy's anger and frustration. For a moment I was amused, but then I realized an enraged Fuzz Boy was even more dangerous. I needed out of here.

"HEELLLLPP!" I shouted out from behind Fuzz Boy's frantically gripping hands.

"No one can hear you, little dude," Zippy said. But he was wrong.

Only a minute or two later a shadow fell across us. Fuzz Boy and I looked up to find a very angry Stench.

My best friend didn't even say a word. He just wound up his arm and punched Fuzz Boy so hard that the creep went flying into a stack of tires over eight feet away. Zippy freaked out and bolted for home. Even at his speed, though, he couldn't evade a long, powerful tongue that shot out and encircled one of his feet. As it was whipped out from under him, he tripped and fell howling into a tangle of used TV antennas.

"Are you okay?" Hal asked me as he helped me to my feet.

"What did he do to me?" I asked in a panic as my hands went for my face. All I could feel, though, was stubble.

"It's just a five o'clock shadow," Stench said. "It's lucky we got here so fast."

"That's just it," I said, "you didn't get here that fast. He was on top of me for three or four minutes. This was the best he could do."

"Fuzz Boy, too?" said Plasma Girl with alarm. "First Lobster Boy, then AI, and now Stench's brother? Maybe this power loss is only happening to nasty people."

"That would be nice," I said as I scratched at the uncomfortable whiskers, "except it happened to my mom and dad this morning. And don't forget Mayor Whitewash."

"It happened to my mom, too," Halogen Boy added

with more than a hint of concern.

"That's just too freaky," Tadpole said. "What's causing this? And how do we stop it from affecting us?"

"I think I know," I announced. "And if I'm right, it's time for us to pay a visit to the one person who can do something about it."

CHAPTER SEVENTEEN

The Hero Reviled

"You're saying that AI's Pseudo-Chips could be what's causing people to lose their powers," Tadpole repeated as we walked toward downtown. Other than a run-in with a particularly slobbery camel, we had so far managed to avoid any dangerous animal encounters.

"The Red Menace himself *told* us that they would be his tool for making everyone the same," I reminded them. "At the time, I had no idea what he could have possibly meant by that, but now it all makes sense."

"It does?" asked Halogen Boy.

"Think about it," I said. "Has anything changed over the past week other than people's constant consumption of these chips?"

"No, everyone is eating them," Stench pointed out. "Except us."

"Thanks to O Boy," Halogen Boy added.

"But that means everyone else is going to lose their powers," Plasma Girl said.

"Unless we get these phony chips off the market," I concluded as we came to a stop outside our destination—Crania-Superiore Hospital. "And there's only one person who can do that."

Passing through the front door, I led us right up to the main nurse's station. A woman with surprisingly wide, vacant-looking eyes was sitting at the desk. I glanced at her nameplate.

"Umm, Nurse Slaphappy?" I cleared my throat. "We're looking for the Amazing Indestructo."

"I'm sorry," she said cheerfully. "No children are allowed in the patients' rooms."

This threw me for a moment, and I instinctively found my fingers tugging at my still-stubbly chin. Then an idea struck!

"Well, clearly you didn't notice"—I spoke again, this time in my deepest possible voice—"the whiskers on my face."

She stared at me blankly, absorbing what I had said.

"Oh!" She brightened up and blinked her eyes. "Of course you can go in, sir. Room one sixty-five. It's just down that hall."

"Wait here, guys," I said with a big grin. "I'll be back as quickly as I can."

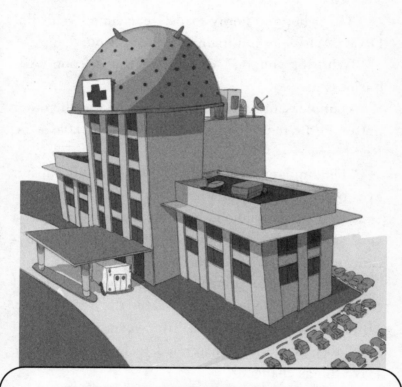

CRANIA-SUPERIORE HOSPITAL

Located on Hoity-Toity Row on the northern edge of Lava Park, Crania-Superiore has become the city's most financially successful hospital thanks to its exclusive focus on diseases of the rich. The hospital is named in honor of an unknown benefactor who has contributed enormous sums expressly for the study of the brain and its functions.

I could tell my friends were annoyed as I left them behind in the lobby, but it would probably be in our best interest for me to do this on my own. Unfortunately, as I stepped into room 165, I saw that I had company anyway.

"Great hoppin' horny toads!" exclaimed Whistlin' Dixie. "Why sure'n if it ain't Ordinary Boy."

"Who let you in?" demanded the Tycoon, AI's business partner.

As unpleasant as it was to see him, it was the other person in the room that made my blood run cold—the Red Menace.

"This midget looks familiar," he said, his sinister eyes boring right through me.

"That's not a midget," said the Tycoon. "It's just a very annoying kid who always seems to know everything except what's good for him."

"Ah, yes, it does appear to be the young boy who I chatted with on Wednesday," observed the Red Menace. "But now he's got a beard. Fifty years ago, before I went to prison, children tended to be clean shaven. Have things changed?"

"That ain't no beard." Dixie laughed as she dropped to one knee to wipe my chin with her hanky. She jerked back in surprise when she found the hairs were real. "Sure'n if he hasn't grown his self a set o whiskers!"

"They'll go away in about an hour," I said to everyone, "just like your powers if you don't take steps now to prevent it."

"What did he say about powers?" I heard a creaky voice from across the room. That was when I noticed the patient in the hospital bed. It was hard to recognize him beneath all the casts and bandages, but even in a weakened state I knew the voice of the Amazing Indestructo.

"It's true," I said speaking directly to AI. "I think the Red Menace is using your Pseudo-Chips to drain everybody's powers—including your own."

"Not my chips!" AI responded plaintively.

"I notice you said you *think* that Pseudo-Chips might be causing this," the Tycoon pointed out. "So the reality is that you don't *know* it for a fact."

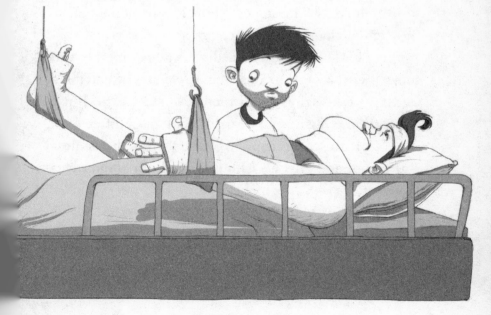

"Well, no," I admitted, "but the link looks pretty strong."

"This here li'l buckaroo may jes' be on to somethin'," said Dixie with concern. "Ah even hit ma self a wrong note this mornin'—in the show'r, no less!"

"Mays, mights, possiblies," the Tycoon said with a snort. "Until you have hard facts, we're certainly not going to pull an item that's bringing in more income for Indestructo Industries than all our past products combined."

"But what good is anything if you have to change your entire way of life to keep using it?" I asked. "Besides, there's only one reason that people are eating these chips."

The Red Menace gave an evil leer as I turned to face him.

"You're right," he agreed. "People buy them because they're delicious. Don't you agree?"

I could tell that he was using his power on me, and somewhere in my subconscious I felt myself craving a canister of Amazing Indestructo Pseudo-Chips. But I knew the feeling was phony and shook myself free of it.

"No I don't," I snapped back. "They're tasteless and bland, and anyone who can think for themselves knows it."

The Red Menace's face turned as red as his

costume, but before he could say anything, a loud sobbing noise drifted through the room. We all turned to
the Amazing Indestructo, who was blubbering like a
baby.

"H-h-he's right!" he wailed uncontrollably. "Even I
think they taste lousy."

"So take them off the market," I appealed directly
to him. "For once do something for the right reason—
even if it costs you some money."

"Money?" he said, his tears ceasing.

The Tycoon saw his opening and went for it.

"That's right," he said in the oiliest way possible.
"If you take these chips off the market you'll be sacri-
ficing uncountable millions in profit. You don't want to
do that, do you?"

"No." AI shook his head vacantly. "I like money."

I couldn't believe it. The Amazing Indestructo and
the Tycoon weren't even under the Red Menace's control. It was their own greed that was driving their actions.

"Is money so important to you that you'd give up
the one thing that makes you unique among everyone
else in Superopolis?" I asked AI in disbelief.

"You mean my profile?" he said as he turned to
show it to me. The huge welt on his nose had done
nothing to improve it.

"No!" I practically exploded. "Your power! Your

indestructibility! What good is your money if you don't have that?!"

The Amazing Indestructo immediately began blubbering again.

"It's true. My power is the only thing that makes me special. Without it people will see that I'm just a two-bit phony."

"A *rich* two-bit phony," the Tycoon corrected as he walked over to the hospital room's door. "Nurse Slaphappy, we need your assistance for a moment."

AI continued to sob as Nurse Slaphappy came into the room. Just as I was wondering what her power might be, the nurse came to the side of the hospital bed and gave the sobbing Amazing Indestructo a solid whack across the face with her hand.

Instead of reacting as most people would when getting slapped, AI began to grin and laugh. Nurse Slaphappy was well named.

With his mood completely lifted, the Amazing Indestructo came up with a solution to this problem that only he could have concocted.

"Wait a minute!" he lit up. "If I were to sell the kid the business, I can have my money and he can do what he wants with the chips. Everyone would win!"

My mouth dropped open at the spinelessness of this hero who only a month ago I had idolized. A similar expression of outrage flashed across the Red Menace's face as well, but I think for another reason—the thought that AI might actually sell the business to me. He shouldn't have worried.

"That's it!" The Amazing Indestructo grinned as Nurse Slaphappy gave him another smack across the face. "The business is yours kid . . . and all for the bargain price of just one billion dollars."

CHAPTER EIGHTEEN

Riches from the Sky

"What do you mean he refused to stop selling them?" Plasma Girl asked with concern while she and my other teammates scrambled to keep up with me as I stormed out of the hospital.

"He did offer to sell me the business, though—for one billion dollars."

"A billion dollars!!" they all said in astonishment.

"We can't even compete with Transparent Girl's twenty-three-cent fish fund," Tadpole said with annoyance.

"I have a hundred and twenty dollars in my college fund," Hal offered. "Is that close?"

"Not really," I said. "But thanks anyway, Hal."

"Why doesn't he just stop selling the chips because it's the right thing to do?" Stench asked in disgust.

"Because he's selfish and greedy," I said by way of explanation.

"How could anyone sacrifice his own power for profits?" Stench shook his head in amazement.

"Because I didn't have absolute proof that the chips are at fault, the Tycoon convinced him to do nothing."

"That's stupid," said Hal. "He could at least stop until we knew for sure."

"What really upsets me," I admitted, "is that I *don't* know for sure. It's only a guess at the moment."

"People start eating the chips. Their powers go away. What more proof do you want?" snorted Tadpole.

"On the surface, it sounds convincing," I agreed, "but there's no solid evidence. We still don't know what *causes* people's power in the first place, and without knowing that, it's incredibly tricky to figure out what would prevent someone's power from working."

"Maybe there's something in the Pseudo-Chips that blocks people's power," Plasma Girl proposed.

"There could be." I shrugged. "But I've looked over the ingredients label. In spite of a dozen or so unpronounceable additives, the chips don't contain anything that hasn't been used in tons of other products."

"Speaking of food loaded with chemicals, I'm starving," Stench announced. "Let's head someplace where we can get something to eat."

"Should we go to Dinky Dogs?" Halogen Boy proposed.

"No. I heard they were overrun by armadillos," Tadpole said. "Let's hit the Cavalcade of Candy, instead."

"Candy for lunch?!" Plasma Girl snapped, clearly appalled. "That's disgusting!"

We all stared at her blankly. Candy for lunch made perfect sense to the rest of us.

"Oh fine." She gave in as we turned and headed for a building shaped like a giant dollop of whipped cream. Kids of all ages were coming and going as we passed through the main entrance of the Cavalcade of Candy. We took a sharp right and made our way up the spiral pathway that ringed the interior of the hollow structure.

We stopped for a moment to watch the Sugar Rush roller coaster whip by. It's just one of the cool attractions inside the Cavalcade of Candy. Another was the complete model of Superopolis built entirely of candy. It's spread out across the whole bottom floor of the place. After the coaster passed, I looked down at the three-dimensional map of the city just as a worker was adding a new detail. It was a model of the S.S. *Befuddlement* made entirely of Popsicle sticks. The worker, an old man with a neatly trimmed beard was carefully placing the ancient wrecked ship on the rock candy shore of MegaManly Beach. While I marveled at how accurate it was, my friends debated their lunch options.

"Let's eat at that new place on the fifth floor—La Dolce Deli," Tadpole suggested. "I've heard their Marzi-Pan Pizza is fantastic."

"Can't we go to the Peppermint Patio?" pleaded Plasma Girl. "They serve delicious peppermint tea!"

She could tell from our expressions she wasn't going to get far with that idea.

"How about Mother Treacle's Kandy Kitchen?" Stench suggested. "Their Peanut Butter Pot Pie in a milk chocolate crust is fantastic—and healthy! I've had dozens of them."

"Healthy?!" Plasma Girl shot back. "They're probably the cause of you being the size you are."

Plasma Girl immediately realized she shouldn't have made a comment like that. Stench was just big—he wasn't fat. But, nevertheless, his expression fell like a butterscotch soufflé.

"Maybe they have had an effect," he mumbled into his chest.

Cause and effect. There were those two words again. Suddenly an idea struck me as if I'd been hit by . . . well . . . a meteor.

"You guys," I said, turning to my other teammates as the excitement rose in my voice, "I think I know how we can come up with a billion dollars."

"It better not involve selling anything door-to-door," Tadpole announced.

"No," I said. "In fact, it may have just dropped right out of the sky."

"Are you crazy?" asked Stench. "A billion dollars?"

"Remember how I said that every effect has a cause? Well, just look at the Carbunkle Mountains down there," I said pointing to the sculpted blocks of chocolate that represented the enormous mountain range encircling Superopolis.

"We all saw how a meteor hit the surface of the planet with such force that it thrust up the entire Carbunkle range," I pointed out.

"No kidding!" Stench said, clearly impressed. "But what's that got to do with getting us a billion dollars?"

"A lot of times meteorites are made out of incredibly valuable materials," I said. "They can be gold, they can be jewels, they can be copper or platinum or a combination of all of the above."

"Or they can just be made out of rock," Tadpole pointed out.

"What have we got to lose?" I asked. "Let's check it out."

"But what happened to the meteorite?" Hal asked.

"Just look," I replied. "You can see the path the meteor must have taken. It clearly made impact first at the spot where Superopolis Harbor now lies."

"He's right," Tadpole agreed. "Look how round the harbor is."

"And then it plunged straight down where the Greenway sits now," I continued. The Greenway was the tree-lined strip of land that separated the eastbound and westbound lanes of Colossal Way. "Along the way, the meteor barreled into the land, forcing the

Carbunkle Mountains up and up and up."

"So it must have come to a stop at the base of the mountains," concluded Plasma Girl.

And there our eyes all came to rest on it—the smooth, sloping mound that sat smack in the middle of Telomere Park at the very base of the mountain range. It was a location we had become very familiar with over the past couple of weeks.

"Crater Hill," I muttered. "That's it! Right below the water tower that Professor Brain-Drain had converted into his time machine. The meteorite is buried beneath Crater Hill."

I knew I was right, and my friends all nodded their heads.

"I think we've found our treasure meteorite. We just have to go get it."

"But how, O Boy," Tadpole asked. "It's buried who knows *how* deep."

"It could take forever to dig down to it," Plasma Girl agreed.

"Who said anything about digging?" I said.

With growing concern, my friends followed the direction of my eyes as they moved north along the base of the Carbunkle Mountains and finally came to rest on the entrance to the mysterious Carlsbark Caverns.

CHAPTER NINETEEN

The Land Beneath the Ground

The next day, the Carbunkle Mountains towered above us as my friends and I stood before the rocky opening that led to the shadowy Carlsbark Caverns. I had a feeling that if there was any way to see what lurked beneath Crater Hill, exploring these caverns would be our best chance.

"Tell us again why we've come here?" Tadpole said with an annoyance that only partly hid his growing nervousness.

"We're here to test my hypothesis," I stated once again.

"Is that like a hippopotamus?" Hal asked.

"It's more like a theory," I said, "just harder to pronounce."

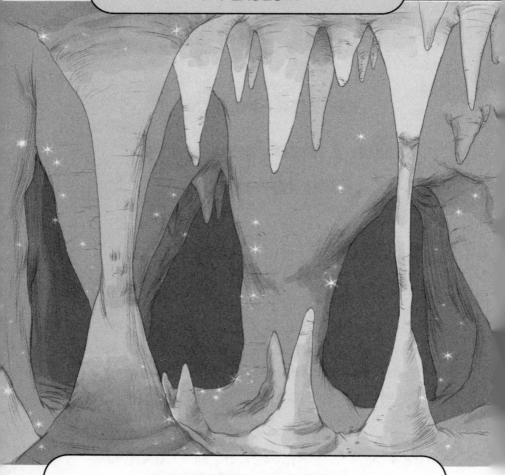

CARLSBARK CAVERNS

Named for the distinct echoes they produce, the Carlsbark Caverns can be accessed only through a single entrance found at the base of the Carbunkle Mountains just north of Telomere Park. The small sections explored thus far have revealed spectacular mineral formations that are dazzling to behold. Even greater wonders—including caverns as vast as three cubic acres—have yet to be discovered.

"And your theory has to do with Crater Hill," Stench said, fishing for the answer.

"Exactly," I responded. "Haven't any of you ever wondered how a hill got a name that makes no sense?"

"Wait a minute. A crater is the exact opposite of a hill," Plasma Girl said as it dawned on her. "You're right, O Boy. That doesn't make any sense at all."

"Unless it once *was* a crater," I pointed out. "And the meteorite is still sitting in it causing the bulge that forms the hill."

"And you think the meteorite could be worth how much?" Stench asked.

"Millions. Or even billions," I said. "Or maybe nothing. But I do know it's the only shot we have of buying out AI and shutting down his Pseudo-Chip operation."

"And you expect us to find it," Tadpole said with a mildly annoyed look on his face.

"Do heroes turn away from a mission?" I asked.

"No," Plasma Girl said with a sigh, "but couldn't a mission sometimes be going to a movie or just baking cookies or something?"

"People are losing their powers," I said, "and this might be the only way to return them."

I stuck out my right fist, thumb extended. Hal

wrapped his right hand around my thumb and Plasma Girl did likewise with his. Stench and Tadpole completed the circle. We were a team.

"Let's go, Junior Leaguers!"

Before anyone could argue, I stepped into the Carlsbark Caverns. I got only about ten feet before the light from the outside began to fade. As the way before me dissolved into darkness, I hesitated.

"Hal, we didn't load you up on apple juice this morning for nothing," I said.

A moment later, Halogen Boy illuminated himself, flooding the caverns with light. What we saw took our breaths away. Stalactites and stalagmites flecked with mica glistened and glittered as shimmering light bounced across cracks and crevices. From somewhere deep within the crevices hidden crystals erupted in jewel-like colors.

"Wow!" Stench and Tadpole said in unison. Plasma Girl and Halogen Boy were awed into silence.

This was the portion of the caverns that most people were familiar with. Every kid in Superopolis had been brought here on a school outing by the time they were in third grade. But this one easily accessible chamber was all that had ever really been explored. There were rumors that the Carlsbark Caverns wound their way through the entire range of the Carbunkle

Mountains, and today I decided it was time for someone to see if it was true.

I plunged ahead and my teammates followed. Hal's light made it easy to pick a path, but Stench still managed to trip over an outcropping of stone and tumble onto the hard floor. Hitting the ground, he produced an all too familiar noise.

"Run for cover!" Tadpole yelled, as we scrambled to escape what we knew was coming. All that came, though, was another noise—a rougher, almost canine version of what Stench had produced. *WOOOFFT!* Followed by *wooft, wooft, wooft.* Finally fading out to a lessening series of *wooft, RUFF, wooft, RUFF.* We were witnessing the famous barking echoes of Carlsbark Caverns. But all we cared about at the moment was avoiding the one unfortunate side effect of Stench's incredible strength.

Tentatively, I sniffed the air around me. To my surprise it smelled fine. My friends followed suit.

"The air is clear," Hal said with more than a little surprise.

"It must have risen up instead of settling down," Plasma Girl guessed.

"I hope it doesn't cause any of those stalactites to fall," Tadpole commented.

"Hey, it wasn't *that* bad," Stench protested.

The words were barely out of his mouth when we heard a rumbling noise high above us. For a moment I thought the ceiling actually *was* falling.

"Bats!!" Plasma Girl screamed before instantly reducing herself to a puddle of goo. As I dived for the ground I felt the first of the panic-stricken creatures brush against the back of my head. I noticed Plasma Girl in her goopy state slithering through a crack between some boulders. Then everything went dark.

Hal had doused his light under the mistaken assumption that the bats couldn't find him if it was dark. Ultimately it didn't matter. They had only one thought in mind and that was to escape the horrendous gas that had risen to their home in the ceiling.

Finally the shrieking, flapping noise ceased, and a few moments later Hal had regained enough nerve to brighten back up. Tadpole immediately turned and glared at Stench, who just shrugged in

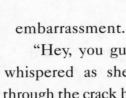

embarrassment.

"Hey, you guys," Plasma Girl whispered as she slithered back through the crack between the boulders and took her normal shape. "You won't believe what's behind here. Stench, can you move these rocks?"

"Of course I can," he said, eager to show the side of his power he was proud of. Effortlessly, he picked up one boulder after another and set them aside. But the more he moved the heavy stones the more difficult it appeared to be getting for him. Finally, with intense concentration on his face, he rolled the final boulder backward to reveal an entry into another dark chamber.

"How were you able to see in there?" I asked Plasma Girl. "It's completely dark."

"Light was coming from somewhere," she said with a shrug.

"Hal," I said, "douse yourself."

The moment Halogen Boy's light vanished, we were all able to see the same thing Plasma Girl had spotted. There was a faint glow

175

coming through an opening set far across and lower down on the other side of this new chamber.

"Now light back up," I instructed Hal, as I kept my eyes glued to the spot. I could no longer see the fainter light once Hal was aglow, but I knew the direction we should go.

Halogen Boy's luminosity revealed a long narrow ledge that sloped downward, always hugging the side of the cavern wall. I led the way forward as we moved in single file along the rocky path. We followed it down and down. Finally, after traveling for over a half hour, and hundreds of feet down, we arrived at the site that Plasma Girl had spotted from across the enormous cavern. The glow she had seen was now noticeable to all of us, and Hal had apparently been reducing his own illumination as this light got stronger.

"You can shut off altogether, Hal," I told him. "The glow is bright enough by itself."

"Huh?" he said in surprise. "Uh, okay, O Boy."

I led us into a long, straight tunnel that went on for several hundred feet and kept getting brighter as I hurried through it. My teammates ran to catch up with me.

Reaching the end of the tunnel I saw that it opened up into a chamber even more enormous than the one we had just come from—only this one was filled with a

brilliant radiance. My mouth dropped open in astonishment at the source of the light. Wedged into the
center of the vast, sprawling chamber was a gigantic—
and glowing—meteorite. It didn't look a day over sixty-
five million years old.

CHAPTER TWENTY

Creepy Crawlies

The chamber in front of us stretched almost a mile across. From the floor of the cavern it was at least a two-hundred-foot rise to the stalactite-covered ceiling. But the immensity of the space itself seemed like nothing compared to the enormous glowing meteorite. The top of it was wedged into the ceiling far above and was no doubt what caused the large, rounded bulge of Crater Hill. I knew that it had to be directly below the water tower in the center of Telomere Park. The bottom portion of the meteorite was submerged in a wide stream that was gurgling its way through the middle of this vast chamber.

What shocked me more than anything else, though, was the meteorite itself. I had been hoping that it might be gold or platinum or maybe even encrusted

with diamonds, emeralds, and rubies. But it was something far more valuable than that. It was, without a doubt, that rarest of all substances—prodigium.

As far as anyone was aware, there had only been one chunk of the element ever discovered. It had been on display in the Superopolis Museum until it was stolen on orders from Professor Brain-Drain. Because of the enormous amount of energy the substance contained, the professor had used it to power his Time Tipler. That original chunk of prodigium had been reduced to a small rock, which I then used to strand him one hundred and thirty million years in the past.

What would he have done if he had known that the very meteor that he was hoping to see destroy Superopolis was in fact a gigantic chunk of prodigium and a storehouse of unlimited power? Thankfully, it was safe from his evil clutches.

"Just look at that!" Tadpole said in amazement.

"It looks just like it did when we last saw it sixty-five million years ago," Stench added. "Or ten days ago, depending on how you look at it."

"It doesn't appear to have lost any of its size," I agreed.

"How did it end up jammed into this huge cavern?" Plasma Girl asked.

"The meteorite itself hasn't budged," I replied.

"The space surrounding it, though, has formed over millions of years by water erosion. See that stream running around the base of the meteorite? Eventually it will wear away enough dirt to make it look like the meteorite is suspended above it."

"The water is the cause and this cavern is the effect," Hal said proudly. I noticed that he wasn't glowing at all despite his pride at mastering my lesson.

"You're right, Hal. And causes that go on for millions and millions of years can produce truly enormous effects like this."

Even as I was saying it my eyes were focusing on something I had just noticed at the base of the meteorite. There was a boat moored in the stream, and it appeared to have a passenger. It was a strange crablike creature and it appeared to be picking away at the part of the meteorite that dipped into the water. Then I noticed there was another one. As my eyes focused, I realized there were dozens of them . . . or was it hundreds?

"What are those things?" Stench whispered from behind me, having just noticed them himself. "And look, there are a bunch of them on the shore, too."

"Eeekk!!" Plasma Girl shrieked as she noticed the strange creatures. "They're disgusting!"

"Not so loud!" I hissed at her. But it was too late. A

dozen or so of the things on shore had stopped what they were doing. They paused, as if waiting for instructions, and then began scurrying in our direction.

"Uh-oh," said Stench. "This can't be good."

"Let's get out of here," I said as I began heading back down the tunnel that had led us into the cavernous chamber. No one was going to argue the point, and they fell in line right behind me.

As we ran, the illumination from the meteorite faded.

"Hal, we need some light," I insisted.

"I'm trying," he said, almost on the verge of tears.

I followed his voice and could vaguely see him fading dimly in and out of view. He had drunk enough apple juice that he should still have plenty of light available. Something was definitely wrong.

"We won't get anywhere in the dark," Plasma Girl wailed. "We'll fall into a chasm and never be seen again."

"What do we do, O Boy?" Stench said, trying to sound calm even though I knew he was worried, too. "I can hear those creatures getting closer."

What *were* we going to do? We were trapped between a treacherous, unlit path ahead of us and some very scary crablike creatures behind us.

"Everybody be quiet," I insisted. "Maybe if they can't hear us, they'll give up and go away."

I knew it was a desperate ploy, but everyone followed my direction. The clicking and clacking of these creature's claws as they scrambled over the rocky floor was now echoing throughout the cave. What *were* these creatures? Their noise got louder and louder until suddenly the sound stopped. For a moment, there was complete silence, except for a slight whimpering right next to me. I knew it was Plasma Girl. I remained silent for over a minute, just listening to her, not knowing what to do.

"Use your power and escape," I finally whispered to her.

"I can't," she answered far too loudly. "It's not working."

The moment she spoke, a cold, sharp claw latched onto my upper arm. I think I may have screamed, but there was no way to tell over the shrieks of my friends. Then another claw grabbed hold of my leg. Within seconds, each of my limbs was immobilized. From the shouts of my friends I could tell they were in the same position. I then felt myself hoisted into the air. A moment later we were moving back in the direction of the meteorite chamber.

The tunnel became brighter and brighter as we moved forward, and I could make out the creatures that had captured us. What I had first taken to be living creatures, I could now see were actually made of metal. These were machines! Where could they possibly have come from? And more important, what were they going to do with us?

For a moment I had a ray of hope that Stench had been able to fight off the creatures and escape. But then I saw that the crabs bringing up the rear had him secured as well. He was struggling but unable to overcome them. My heart sank. If Stench couldn't break free, what chance did any of us have?

"Help! Help!" Tadpole screeched. "Let go of me, you metal misfits."

What really surprised me was how big the creatures actually were. From a distance, I had guessed they were maybe a foot long, a foot wide, and a foot high. In reality they must have been three times that size!

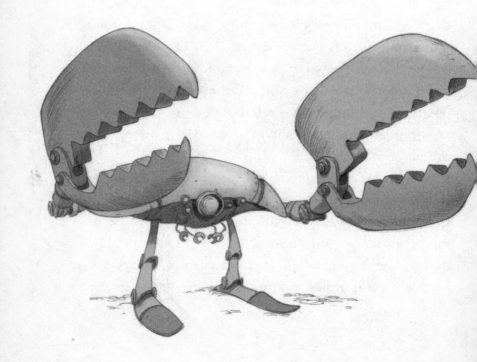

As they carried us down the slope of the cavern and onto the chamber floor, I had a chance to stare ahead at the main mass of metal monsters. They were clustered alongside the stream. Only then did I notice a human figure standing amid them.

"O Boy! What are we going to do?!" Plasma Girl cried out in fear. "I can't get away from these things."

Whatever fear she was feeling couldn't possibly compare to the chill that ran down my spine as I realized we were being delivered into the waiting clutches of Professor Brain-Drain himself.

CHAPTER TWENTY-ONE

A Fiendish Plot

How Professor Brain-Drain had managed to return from one hundred and thirty million years in the past was a mystery that seemed of minor importance at the moment. He had us in his power—at precisely the same instant that my friends had lost the use of theirs.

"Well, now, what have my Crush-staceans found?" he asked with a malevolent chuckle. "I believe I recognize this crop of junior do-gooders." His eyes wandered from one of my friends to another before finally coming to rest on me. "And here's the most meddlesome of all."

"How did you escape?" I demanded as I struggled in vain against the metallic crablike creature that held me captive. "You should still be stranded in the past."

"Yes, I should be." He smiled enigmatically. "But

that's only if one assumes I was ever there to begin with."

"I know you were," I asserted. "I sent you there."

"Indeed you almost did," he said, glaring at me. "And you would have succeeded if it hadn't been for the emergency escape hatch I had installed in the interior of my Time Tipler."

"Escape hatch?" I replied dumbly, feeling somehow I had been cheated.

"Yes," he replied dryly. "No genius leaves himself without an exit plan. Nevertheless, I hesitated before using it, and only barely escaped before the Tipler did its thing."

"Why would you have hesitated?" I asked even as I realized the answer on my own.

"Because, by leaving the Tipler, I, too, could have been destroyed by this approaching meteor." His hand swung up to indicate the enormous mass of prodigium mounted above us. "It took me a moment to make a calculated decision. Surely you know what that was."

"Yes," I grudgingly admitted. "You had to decide if you were in a worse position facing the meteor or being stranded one hundred and thirty million years in the past."

"Correct." He beamed. "And do you know ultimately

why I chose to stay with the endangered citizens of Superopolis?"

"Because it would have been very boring for someone determined to destroy civilization to be stuck in a time before people even existed?" I hazarded a guess.

"Well, no." He shook his head. "Not that your point isn't valid. But my main reason was I had faith in *your* ability to figure out a way to save Superopolis and return it—and me—to the present."

"What??!" I said, both appalled yet oddly pleased.

"Oh, don't pretend to be so modest," he poohpoohed. "You're well aware that you don't possess the same empty shell of a head as most of the residents of this city."

"But what are you doing down here?" I asked. "I mean, with this meteorite?"

"Ah, yes." He clucked. "You, of course, have also recognized it as prodigium, haven't you?"

"Only as we entered this chamber," I admitted. "I never suspected before we came here."

"Really?" said the Professor, "then what possessed you to take this dangerous trek under the mountains? Something must have provoked your curiosity."

"I was curious if anything remained of the meteorite after sixty-five million years," I said, determined not to reveal my treasure hunt scheme. In truth, I wondered what the value of this meteorite might even be.

Prodigium was considered priceless when nobody thought any existed. What it was worth in huge supply was anyone's guess. And what kind of effects might this much prodigium be having on the people of Superopolis? I was beginning to get a whopper of an idea.

"Well, let me tell you why I am here," he said as he lapsed into the habit of every villain of explaining himself. "I had always been aware that a meteor impact created the topographical features of Superopolis. And long ago I was able to calculate exactly when it had happened, thanks to my analysis of the rock strata and soil erosion patterns of the Carbunkle Mountains. But I always assumed that the meteor itself had been obliterated upon impact. I never imagined that it could have been made up of pure prodigium until I saw it in person. In those last few minutes while you were saving the city, I was observing its approach from my hiding spot. I was astounded to see that it was, indeed, prodigium—a substance I always thought to be practically nonexistent."

"I remember," I said. "You waited twenty-five years for me to return with the one small chunk that you needed to operate the Tipler."

"Exactly. So just imagine the marvelous ideas I've gotten as I've thought about what I could do with a million times as much of the power-packed substance."

"I shudder to think . . ." I started to say.

"You should," he replied, as his eyebrows scrunched menacingly. "Because it also has occurred to me that this much power could very well be the answer to a mystery that has baffled me my entire life. . . . Could it be the cause of the unique powers of every citizen of Superopolis?"

I couldn't hide my sharp intake of breath. "See?" I turned to my captive friends. "He thinks powers are caused by something, too!"

"O Boy," Plasma Girl replied with disgust, "he's an evil villain. I would hardly point to him as support for your theory."

"Of course powers are caused by something," the Professor said dismissively. "Everything has a cause. And this meteorite—this gargantuan chunk of prodigium—must somehow be radiating *its* power in the creation of *our* powers."

I was so disturbed over the fact that Professor Brain-Drain and I had been thinking along identical lines once again that I almost missed his next statement.

"That is why I must now destroy it."

"What?!" I said. Looks of horror appeared on my friends' faces. If the Professor was right, and he succeeded in his plan, it would be devastating for them.

"Why would you do that?" I asked in alarm.

"Because I can," he replied matter-of-factly. "I've

190

deduced that it must be the water streaming around the base of the meteorite that is actually being affected. As it flows out of the mountains, it then enters the Superopolis water supply. For a week now, my trusty Crush-staceans have been chipping away at the base of the meteorite. Soon it will be completely clear of the stream. Even now the effects must be beginning to be felt throughout the city."

I wasn't going to give him the satisfaction of confirming that he was right, but as he looked at my helpless friends and gave a knowing smirk, I knew he already had all the proof he needed.

"In a matter of hours they will have removed all of it that intrudes into the river," he continued. "Once they have, the water in this chamber will cease to provide its benefit, and the citizens of Superopolis will be left bereft of their powers."

"But what about you?" I pointed out. "You'll lose your power as well."

"What would you say if I told you I lost my power over ten years ago?" He smiled cryptically.

"Huh?" I said in astonishment. "But I know that's not true."

"Do you?" The Professor pushed the point. "Have you ever seen me actually drain anybody's brain?"

I went silent as I thought back over my previous

meetings with the Professor. He was right. I never had seen him actually use his power. He *had* used his Brain Capacitor to drain away the intelligence of a number of victims. This included the actors who had played him on TV, all of whom were turned into Dumbots.

"But you've tried draining my own brain a bunch of different times," I countered.

"Tried, yes," he admitted, "but never succeeded."

"If you have no power, why try at all?" I asked.

"When one is perpetrating a charade, it's important to play along with the game," he replied. "People believed I could drain their brains because I acted as if I could. In the meantime, I developed alternative methods to achieve the same effect."

"Like the Brain Capacitor and the Oomphlifier?" I asked.

"Exactly," he replied. "Thankfully, I retained all the intelligence I had absorbed during the years my power was effective, and I used that intelligence to find a solution to my dilemma. The Brain Capacitor, which you children almost had a chance to experience, is a mechanical version of my own power. It can sap the intelligence of anyone I strap into it. The problem is that it's the size of a cement truck and isn't very practical outside my laboratory."

"And the Oomphlifier?"

"I invented a power-magnification device under the assumption that I could restore my power by amplifying it," he said as he reached over to a pitcher of water that was sitting on a nearby table. It was full of ice cubes. "That, too, failed to achieve its primary goal."

I cringed at the thought that I had tried to use the Oomphlifier for the exact same purpose.

"I even modified the colander on my head with the controls necessary to mentally direct my mechanical creations," he added as he silently instructed the Crush-staceans to lower us to the ground while still keeping our limbs immobile. "In ten years I've discovered thousands of ways to extract, store, and manipulate brain power. I just haven't figured out how to reinstate my original power—until now!"

An involuntary shudder ran through my body as the Professor picked up a glass and began pouring himself some water.

"You may all be wondering why I revealed something so personal." He chuckled as he filled his glass and set the pitcher down. It was only then that I noticed that what I had thought were ice cubes floating in the water were actually small chunks of prodigium. "The reason is that you won't possess that knowledge for very long. You will, however, have the honor of being the first victims to have your brains drained the old-fashioned way in over a decade."

He took one drink out of the glass of water before setting it back down and then confidently approached me as I struggled against the steely claws of the Crush-stacean.

"It truly is a pity," was all he said as his finger reached out and came to rest on my forehead.

CHAPTER TWENTY-TWO

Escape from the Caverns

Oddly, nothing happened. At least I didn't think anything was happening. I certainly didn't feel myself getting dumber. The Professor's face was wrinkling in annoyance. He lifted his finger and then once again pressed it against my skull. Still nothing. Professor Brain-Drain's face twisted into a snarl as he began repeatedly poking me in the head.

"Stop that!" I finally blurted out in irritation.

"Aaarrrgghhh!" he erupted in a howling cry of frustration.

"Maybe this meteorite isn't the source of everyone's power," I suggested.

"Of course it is," he shouted back. "I clearly just need more exposure to it to restore my ability. Besides, you kids confirmed that my plan to eliminate the powers of everyone else has already begun working."

"I'm not so sure," I said. "We also think that the Red Menace might be using his new potato chips to accomplish the same thing."

"The Red Menace?!" Professor Brain-Drain reacted with alarm. "I drained the Red Menace of his intelligence ten years ago. He shouldn't be able even to tie his shoes."

"Maybe your power worked as well on him as it did on me," I proposed.

"You're in no position to be tweaking me, boy," Professor Brain-Drain hissed menacingly. "If people are losing their powers, it's because of what I'm doing to this meteorite."

"Maybe. Maybe not." I shrugged. "The Red Menace has used his power to convince everyone to switch to these bland Pseudo-Chips that the Amazing Indestructo is producing. And since everybody started eating them, powers have begun to vanish. Even AI has lost his power."

"Really?" Professor Brain-Drain perked up warily. "The imbecile is no longer indestructible? What a delightful development! Who else has been affected?"

"You really need to get out and buy a newspaper," I suggested. "It started with just a few people, but it appears to be spreading. Mayor Whitewash is calling for calm, but no one is listening to him anymore."

"Indeed?" Professor Brain-Drain lit up even further at this comment. He was recovering rapidly from his earlier disappointment. "He's lost his power, too. That can't bode well for the buffoon with an election drawing near."

"His only opponent is a pumpkin," I informed him. "I think his job is safe."

"Don't be so certain." The Professor began to chuckle. "You've given me a marvelous idea."

"Well, since your mood has improved so much, could it possibly involve letting us go?" I asked, not really expecting a yes to that question.

"Oh, definitely not," he replied cheerfully. "You know far too much. And since I can't yet drain that knowledge from your brains, I'll have to find another way of silencing you."

I don't know what Professor Brain-Drain's "another way" was going to be, since the very moment the words left his mouth, a tongue—a very long and unexpected tongue—lashed out, wrapped itself around one of the handles of his colander, and yanked it right off the Professor's head. The second his method for controlling the Crush-staceans was gone, the claws that held me and my teammates opened. We didn't waste the opportunity.

"Run for it!" I hollered as Professor Brain-Drain howled in frustration.

"Tadpole, you still have your power," Plasma Girl said with an outpouring of relief as she watched him whip the stainless steel strainer at least fifty yards away.

"Yeah, and I'm glad I kept it a secret," he responded as he reeled in his tongue. "Now let's get out of here."

"But how?" Stench asked. "Brain-Drain will be back in control of those crab things before we can escape."

"I have an idea," I shouted. "Quick, over this way."

I led my teammates toward one of the rowboats that the Crush-staceans were using to haul away the chunks of meteorite they chipped off. One of the small boats had just been unloaded and we all jumped into it.

"Stench, I hope you have enough strength left to row us out to the middle of this stream," I said. "You need to get us there, and fast."

Back on shore Professor Brain-Drain was rushing to retrieve his colander. Even as Stench picked up the speed of his stroke, I saw the Professor place his stainless steel headgear back atop his noggin. Seconds later, the Crush-staceans regained life. Just as they began to move toward us, I felt the strong central current grab hold of the boat, and we were soon rushing away from the cavern. There was no need to even row, and an exhausted Stench stopped trying.

Back on the shore, Professor Brain-Drain jumped up and down in a rage.

We didn't have long to savor our victory, however. The speed of the river was increasing dramatically, and we soon found ourselves being whisked toward a dark, low hanging cave that the entire river was rushing into.

"HELLLLP!!" Plasma Girl screamed. And then her voice dropped away dramatically, and I felt us plummet into nothingness. If only I could see!

As if in answer to my wish, our boat burst out of the darkness and into a different chamber that was bright with phosphorescent crystals. The river was so narrow now that it was moving at a frightening speed. The channel that the river had dug over millions of years twisted one way and then another; left to right; backward and forward.

"I think I'm gonna puuuuuke," Tadpole wailed.

A moment later we shot out of the chamber and into a tunnel with concrete walls. We were now someplace man-made. The important thing was we had escaped the Carlsbark Caverns.

Our boat began to slow, and when I saw a stone ledge protruding slightly into the stream, I instructed Stench to take up the oars again and maneuver us toward it. He succeeded but not without difficulty.

"Where are we?" Plasma Girl asked nervously as we got out of the boat.

"My guess is that this is the Superopolis water supply," I answered. "If we kept going, I'm sure we would end up in the Ornery Ocean."

"No thanks," Tadpole said with a snort. "But how do we get out of here?"

I figured this must be some sort of maintenance platform, which meant there had to be an exit nearby. I began feeling around and soon found the steel rung of a ladder.

"Here we go," I said. "It's time for a climb."

And climb we did. It felt like we scaled hundreds of feet before I finally bumped my head against a metal plate that I managed to budge free. We clambered up through a manhole and found ourselves in the middle of the Greenway.

I looked back at Crater Hill, now off in the distance. It was no longer a mystery to me how it had gotten its name. And then it hit me. How *did* it get its name? No one, at least until now, had had any idea that the hill was formed by a meteorite resting in a sixty-five-million-year-old crater. Or so I had assumed. But whoever had given the hill its name had obviously known as well. The question was already gnawing at me. Who could that person have been?

CHAPTER TWENTY-THREE

Normalopolis

The moment I arrived at school on Monday, I knew that the powers outage had spread to nearly everyone. Even Tadpole had lost his power.

"I just woke up this morning like this," he said panic-stricken as he kept trying to stick out his tongue. It went no farther than anybody else's.

"It has affected all of us," Plasma Girl added with concern in her voice. "But why? We stopped eating AI's Pseudo-Chips days ago! Maybe Professor Brain-Drain *is* behind everybody's power loss."

"I just don't know," I said, truly baffled. "We have two major supervillains, either of whom could be responsible for this catastrophe. But if it's the Red Menace, none of you should be affected. And if Professor Brain-Drain is correct, his power should be fully functional, yet it's not."

"My head hurts just thinking about it," Halogen Boy fretted.

"They can't both be right," I whispered under my breath. "But on the other hand they may not both be wrong."

I was still trying to put *that* idea together as we entered the classroom and found a scene I never would have thought possible.

It was a room full of completely *ordinary* kids. The Human Sponge's head was no longer porous— although the skin she had now looked like it was headed for trouble in the acne department. Somnia was fully awake. Cannonball kept bumping up against the Quake as if he was trying to knock her over. And she kept hitting him back, but with nothing even close to the bone-rattling power she used to be able to muster. It *was* sort of enjoyable watching the two creeps beating each other up.

Puddle Boy was no longer creating puddles under his desk. Instead, he was producing one on top of it. Only this time it was just ordinary tears as he bemoaned the loss of a power that, if I were him, I'd be happier without.

Lobster Boy actually seemed a little relieved, which I guess made sense now that he knew he had company.

Even as Sparkplug tried in vain to poke him with an electrical charge, he just sat there unfazed.

"All the fizz has gone out of my life!" I heard Little Miss Bubbles complain to Plasma Girl as we took our seats. She did in fact look drab and dispirited, without a hint of bubbliness about her—assuming that's even a word.

"I feel the same," Plasma Girl said as she sat down.

"Hey, who's the new kid?" Tadpole asked. A boy we had never seen before entered the room and walked over to the far row where he took a seat in front of a very unlimber-looking Limber Lass. "He's taking Foggybottom's seat."

"I think that *is* Foggybottom," I replied. "We've just never gotten a good look at him when he wasn't encased in a cloud."

On his right sat Transparent Girl, who I could also see well for the very first time. She turned toward me and my eyes went wide. Despite the worry on her face, Transparent Girl was—surprisingly—pretty! Her behavior has always been so nasty that I just assumed she was as unattractive as her personality. I couldn't help but stare at this unexpected revelation.

"What are you gawking at?" I heard Plasma Girl's voice a fraction of a second before her hand smacked me alongside the head. "Just because you can see her now doesn't mean she won't still try every underhanded trick in the book to beat you in next week's election."

Thankfully, Melonhead arrived just then causing a distraction. To my amazement, he didn't look the least bit different.

"Greethingth, voterth," he said without enthusiasm. There was no spray of juice or seeds. Yet he was still shaped like a melon and had the markings of a watermelon running vertically up to the rounded point of his head. I guess that his appearance was just a natural part of who he was.

Miss Marble followed right behind him, looking grumpier than I had ever seen her. She took her seat and then something miraculous happened. We all became quiet, waiting for her to speak. She was as surprised as anyone.

"Well, something has finally occurred to leave you kids tongue-tied," she said. The moment the words were out of her mouth, the spell was broken. Practically every student in class raised his or her hand and began shouting questions simultaneously.

"What happened to our powers?" shrieked Transparent Girl. "We've lost them just when we need them most to protect ourselves from all these crazy animals."

"I don't feel right," protested the Spore, who, for

NAME: Miss Marble. **POWER:** The ability to cast a paralyzing spell over living subjects. **LIMITATIONS:** Paralysis lasts only a few minutes. **CAREER:** A desire for low pay and little respect led her to teaching. **CLASSIFICATION:** Chronically annoyed.

the first time ever, had a healthy pink glow to his skin.

"No one can hear me!" I barely heard the Banshee whimper.

"We're all like Ordinary Boy," Cannonball wailed. I knew he had meant that as an insult, but I actually enjoyed the howl of despair in his voice.

"Calm down, kids," Miss Marble urged, despite no sense of calm in her own voice. "Someone is bound to figure out what is causing our loss of power and correct it soon. We just need to be patient. In the meantime, let's try to concentrate on our lessons. Everybody take out your biology books and we'll continue our discussion of the anatomy of the potato fungus."

Only the Spore perked up at that suggestion.

"Miss Marble!" My hand shot up. "Could we talk about history instead this morning?"

"Again with the history," she said. "Why would we discuss that? It's already happened, so what's the point?"

"Maybe if we knew something about past events, it might give us an idea today for solving this power crisis," I proposed. For once nobody shouted my idea down.

"I don't see how," she said.

"Well, think about it," I said. "Nobody seems to know how long Superopolis has even existed. When was it settled? And by whom? And did they have powers when they got here?"

"There he goes again, Miss Marble," Transparent Girl said, pointing a finger at me. "Ordinary Boy is claiming that our powers aren't an unchangeable part of us."

"Your complaint would have more validity, Transparent Girl, if it weren't for the fact that currently everyone's power is very much a changeable part of who they are." Miss Marble actually stuck up for me. "Like it or not, you have, in fact, become normal. Go on, Ordinary Boy."

"That's a perfect example!" I blurted out. "Take the word 'normal.' It means average. It's used to describe something that is just like everything else. But here we are saying that people have turned 'normal,' as if that was the natural state. Why would we be using the word in that way unless at one time everyone really *was* normal? Take my own name for instance. I'm called 'ordinary' but there's nobody else like me. I'm ordinary compared to whom?!"

"You're ordinary compared to everybody!" Cannonball snorted. A week ago he would have gotten the laugh he expected from that line, but now nobody found it particularly funny.

"I see your point," Miss Marble said as she considered the logic of what I had said. "But how would we even figure out what life was like for people over a hundred years ago? They're all gone."

"But they've left clues behind. Like the names

that they gave to places," I added, remembering my question from yesterday about Crater Hill. "And there must be physical things, too."

"If a man-made item ith two hundred yearth old," Melonhead spoke up, "it mutht mean that people were here two hundred yearth ago."

"Melonhead is right," I said, almost choking on the words. "So all we have to do is figure out what the oldest object is in Superopolis."

Every kid in my class went silent and stared directly at Miss Marble.

"I'm not *that* old," she blurted out in annoyance. "Think again."

Everyone began shouting out suggestions.

"There's a seven-year-old jar of tartar sauce in my refrigerator," said the Spore as he licked his lips just thinking about it.

"My grandma has a fruitcake that she's been setting out at holidays for twenty years," volunteered Limber Lass.

"My dad just turned forty-three," hollered the Quake.

For lack of any practical suggestions, everyone tried outdoing everybody else. They were coming up with increasingly older items—only none of them was useful.

The noise reached a peak as Transparent Girl attempted to top the whole class.

"The Carbunkle Mountains are sixty-five million years old," she shouted, ignoring the fact that we were looking for something man-made. "We all saw how they got here."

The arguments among my classmates continued to build and Miss Marble was just getting frustrated. Her power was gone, too, and she had no way to rein in the class. But I was no longer paying attention. I had just realized what the oldest thing in Superopolis actually was.

CHAPTER TWENTY-FOUR

On the S.S. Befuddlement

"I still don't see what you're getting at," Stench said as we left school at the end of the day. "What difference does it make knowing when Superopolis was settled?"

"And how would we find out, anyway?" Tadpole added.

"Well, it only stands to reason that the oldest man-made object in Superopolis has something to do with the first people here," I explained. "And Transparent Girl gave me the clue I needed to figure out what that is."

"How did she do that?" Hal asked, tilting his head in confusion.

"When she brought up the Carbunkle Mountains, she added that we all knew how they got here," I said. "She meant the meteorite that created them, of course, but it made *me* wonder how did the *people* of Superopolis get here?"

"I don't see—" Stench started to say.

"Yes, you do," I corrected him. "You see it every time we go to the beach."

They looked at me with blank expressions.

"The lighthouse on Hero's Cape?" asked Stench.

"I've worked there a couple of times," Halogen Boy agreed. "It *is* really old."

"Yes, but not the oldest thing on the beach," I corrected. "Whoever built the lighthouse first had to get here. And how would they have gotten here . . . ?"

"Probably by sea—" Plasma Girl started to say.

"The wreck of the S.S. *Befuddlement*!" Stench beat her to it.

The S.S. *Befuddlement* was an enormous ship that had run aground on the south shore of MegaManly Beach. It was a rocky part of the seashore, so most people never went anywhere near it. Even from a distance, though, it was easy to see how old it was. But it wasn't until now that I realized the potential significance of its age.

"Exactly!" I beamed. "And we're going to investigate it, to see what clues it may hold to the origin of Superopolis itself."

"This isn't going to be as dangerous as our visit to the Carlsbark Caverns, is it?" asked Plasma Girl. "With no powers, we're going to have to be careful."

THE S.S. *BEFUDDLEMENT*

Despite the mystery of its origins, the wreck of this once-mighty sailing vessel, which sits along the southeastern shore of Superopolis Harbor, is seldom visited by the residents of Superopolis. If they were to take a look, they would find more questions raised than answered. So it's probably good they don't, since that kind of thing just annoys people.

"Don't worry," I said. "This should be perfectly safe—assuming we don't run into a kangaroo with death-ray eye beams or something like that."

I'm not completely sure I had put them at ease, but they followed me anyway through the lower Superopolis shopping area and then into the heart of the downtown office district. As we passed under the shadow of the Vertigo Building, I gave a small shudder at the thought that Professor Brain-Drain was still out there some-where. He may not have his power, but he was still an evil genius.

We were soon on South Harbor Drive and followed it all the way out to where it came to an end at the ocean. Jogging down the sandy slopes and onto the beach, we looped around to the left. As soon as we rounded an outcropping of dunes and grasses, we came upon the wreck of the S.S. *Befuddlement*.

"It's as long as a football field!" Tadpole said with awe.

"And you were right about it being ancient," Stench added.

It *was* an old ship. There was no denying that. Even the old fishing trawler that Cap'n Blowhole piloted looked modern in comparison. You could see that at one time the ship had had four enormous masts, but two of them were now long gone. This was a craft that had been powered by the wind alone. As we got closer, it became apparent that this ship had been sitting here for decades—possibly even *centuries*. The wood was decaying and there was an enormous hole torn into the side of it.

Cautiously I led my teammates up to the wide opening.

"Should we go inside?" I asked, turning to my friends.

"When have we ever not gone into a situation that looked potentially dangerous," Plasma Girl said with a sigh as I stepped in through the gaping hole.

The first thing I noticed was the enormous holds in the lower level of the ship. It was clear that this ship had carried an awful lot of something.

"There are some steps over here," Halogen Boy called out. "They go up into the ship."

We all went over to where Hal was standing and inspected the stairs. They looked pretty solid, but I carefully made my way to the top before motioning my teammates to follow. While I waited for them, I inspected this new level of the ship. I was in a large open area with blackboards on the walls, display cases mounted on counters, and work tables littered with shards of glass. And then I thought I heard someone step on a piece of glass farther ahead in the darkness.

"What is this place?" Plasma Girl asked as she came up behind and spooked me.

"It looks like a laboratory that no one has used for a couple hundred years," I answered, deciding she must have made the noise. "But why would a ship have a laboratory?"

"And what was kept in those holds?" Stench added. He, Hal, and Tadpole had just joined us.

"What else is on this ship?" I asked no one in particular as I continued our exploration.

We soon found another stairway and made our way up it. This took us to a level of cabins. There were hundreds of them.

The interior of the ship was in far better shape than the exterior, and we continued to find stairwells. Making our way up another three levels, we at last found ourselves on the deck of the ship. This of course had been fully exposed to the elements and was in horrible condition. We were incredibly careful as we made our way across it toward a large cabin at the stern of the ship.

I hadn't taken more than a half dozen steps toward it when my foot plunged through a rotten board.

"Help!!" I yelled as I frantically grabbed hold of another plank to keep from falling to the deck below. "But be careful."

As Tadpole inched his way toward me, I glanced

down into the space below me. I heard a quiet creak and then I swear I saw a figure darting into the shadows.

"You gotta watch your step, O Boy," Tadpole said as he hauled me to my feet. "This place is a disaster."

I didn't even know how to respond, I was so distracted by what I thought I had seen. Despite lots more creaking boards and a couple other close calls, we slowly made our way to the door of the cabin. Swinging it open, we found the faded remnants of what must have at one time been a spectacular home for the captain of this ship. Even rotted as it was, the wood inside still had a lingering richness to it. Shards of glimmering colored glass remained in half the windows. Everything else appeared to have been stripped from the room, with the exception of an enormous mahogany desk that sat in the center. Moving behind it, I reached for the desk's center drawer and gave it a tug. At first it didn't budge, and I tried again with more force. This time it jerked open with a loud, wood-against-wood scraping sound. Sitting inside the drawer was a single book.

"What is it?" Plasma Girl asked eagerly.

"It appears to be the ship's log," I answered as I flipped it open.

"It looks like a book to me," Hal said.

"A ship's log *is* a book," I explained as I carefully turned the pages. "It records all the details of a ship's voyage, including its cargo."

"What does it say?" Stench pressed me as I scanned the entries.

"It's incredible," I responded. "This ship had everything. Hundreds of species of plants and animals, and—"

"And what?" Tadpole pressed as I paused in astonishment.

"Potatoes," I finally replied. "Tons and tons of potatoes."

That was baffling enough, but then I flipped to a

page that included a passenger list and my eyes went wide with shock.

"What do you see?" Plasma Girl insisted. "Tell us!"

"It's the passengers on the ship," I explained. "But the names are unlike any I've ever seen. They all have two, or sometimes even three names—and none of them indicate what these people's powers were."

And then I saw a name I recognized. My friends all caught the shock that spread across my face.

"What is it?" Plasma Girl pressed. "Whose name do you see?"

"It's someone I never even thought existed." I swallowed. "But here it is, plain as day—Dr. Ambrose . . . Telomere."

CHAPTER TWENTY-FIVE

A New Candidate

"But I didn't think there was a Dr. Telomere," Halogen Boy said in confusion as we left the ship.

"I didn't either," I said. "Even my dad always insisted he was just a made-up advertising character."

"That ship is ancient," added Plasma Girl. "Even if there was a Dr. Telomere, he's long gone now."

As we went on and on about what we had found, we climbed back up the dunes and hills until we reached the street. Once there, we couldn't help but notice the large crowds of people, all headed toward nearby Tremor Park. Tremor Park wasn't as vast as Telomere Park, and it didn't have the attraction of a live volcano like Lava Park, but it did have a feature neither of those could claim. Just take a look at its entry in the *Li'l Hero's Handbook* and you'll see what I mean.

TREMOR PARK

From its scenic perch overlooking the Ornery Ocean, Tremor Park provides some of the city's most stunning views. But it gets its name from its most startling feature. Without warning, seismic shocks regularly roll through the park, often with amusing results. Picnickers are warned that they may end up with more of their lunches on them than in them.

It was against this scenic backdrop that Mayor Whitewash had chosen to hold his latest campaign rally. What had looked to be another uncontested victory for the mayor had now turned into a real race. The carved pumpkin he had faced a week earlier at his debate was now polling almost even with him.

"Thank you all for coming, fellow Superopolopolites," he announced with an air of desperation that only a man tied in popularity with a giant gourd could muster. "I know that everyone is upset about these sudden attacks by superpowered animals."

"And what exactly are you doing about it?" shouted a man wearing a fez and a bathrobe.

"And more important, what are you doing about our vanished powers?" hollered a woman wearing a green leotard with six empty, floppy sleeves.

"Trust me, Madam Octopus," the mayor insisted, "I'm doing everything in my power to solve this mystery."

But that was the problem. Mayor Whitewash's power was long gone. As we had seen at the zoo, no one was buying a word he was saying—a dangerous development for any politician.

"This is obviously the work of some unspeakable villain," he continued, "and I won't rest until we bring this scoundrel to justice and reverse these disturbing effects."

"Perhaps it takes a villain to catch a villain," an unmistakable voice boomed out of nowhere.

My team and I recognized it instantly, but before we could react, the ground itself began to buckle and shake. This wasn't one of Tremor Park's usual hiccups, though. Suddenly, the grassy area in front of the mayor's podium collapsed in on itself creating a gaping hole. The crowd screamed in panic as a swarm of metallic creatures emerged from the earth. With them they brought the sinister figure of Professor Brain-Drain.

"You've failed, Mayor," he stated as he stepped off the Crush-stacean that was carrying him. The metal creatures surrounded the stage as Professor Brain-Drain made his way onto it, a single finger wagging accusingly. "And now it's time for you to pay the price."

The audience gasped as Professor Brain-Drain pressed his finger against Mayor Whitewash's fore-head. The mayor let out a remarkably undignified scream, but then fell silent. As the Professor lowered his finger, I could see from the baffled look on Mayor Whitewash's face that he had just gone through the same experience I had in the Carlsbark Caverns. Only this time Professor Brain-Drain was purposely playing up the result.

"That's right," the villain said to the startled crowd.

"I, too, have lost my power. Whatever has caused this great powers outage has affected me as well."

He looked directly at me and smirked, clearly pleased that he had created an excuse for his own powerlessness before I could reveal it myself.

"So the question I have for you is a simple one," he continued. "Do you want a mayor whose only talent up to now has been the ability to convince you all to overlook his shortcomings and incompetence? Or do you want a mayor who will solve the mystery of our missing powers?"

If the audience looked confused, it was nothing compared to the look of surprise on Mayor Whitewash's face.

"What are you saying?" he began to splutter.

"What I am saying is that I am officially announcing my candidacy for Mayor of Superopolis." Professor Brain-Drain shouted with great fanfare, "Citizens of Superopolis! Give me power, and I will return yours!"

I could tell he was expecting a huge roar of support from the audience, but instead all he got was a skeptical silence.

"Haven't you attempted to destroy all of us a dozen times?" asked one man.

"You obviously haven't been keeping count," the Professor responded indignantly. "I've tried to destroy all of you on seventy-eight different occasions."

"So why help us now?" asked a female hero wearing a jeweled turban.

"A fair question," Professor Brain-Drain admitted. "The truth is that there is no challenge in conquering a city of powerless individuals. Anyone could do that. My goal is to return your powers—as well as my own—so that I may renew my quest to destroy you all."

"Well, that thar makes sense," responded a hero known as the Cowpoke. "It's downright refreshin' to hear a politician respond honestly."

"Professor Brain-Drain's plans may ultimately lead to my complete destruction," proclaimed another woman, "but I can't help but admire his unflinching devotion to his beliefs."

"Are you all crazy?!" I finally erupted as the crowd parted so that everyone could see me. "Professor Brain-Drain is a convicted criminal—not to mention an evil genius."

Thankfully, this caused the crowd to pause and think.

"That's right," someone pointed out, "I'll bet the Professor thinks he's smarter than us."

"Are you one of those people who think you know more than the rest of us?" another man demanded of the Professor. "We don't need any self-styled genius to manage the complex functions of the most essential aspects of our government."

"Vote for me! I don't know anything," blurted out Mayor Whitewash in a pathetic attempt to regain the support of the crowd. Everyone ignored him.

Professor Brain-Drain smiled cryptically. "You're absolutely correct in your skepticism of smart people. What have the few of them in our society ever done for us other than create our technology, produce our art, and unlock the secrets of science?"

"Exactly!" harrumphed the man in the fez.

"Fear not," Professor Brain-Drain continued. "Neither of this lad's scurrilous charges is true. First of all, I have never been convicted of a crime nor spent a moment in jail."

"How could that be?!" I accused.

"Look it up. You'll see that it's true," he dismissed.

I turned to a reporter from *The Superopolis Times*, who was standing right next to me. "Are you going to investigate that claim?" I asked.

"I don't need to." He shrugged. "The Professor himself just said it was true."

Even as my mouth dropped open in astonishment, Professor Brain-Drain continued. "Second, with the loss of my power, I have also lost much of my intelligence," he lied. "In a way it is a blessing. I now see the world from the perspective of a typical ignoramus and I can finally see how wrong it was for me to assume that my massive intelligence somehow made me smarter than you—the decent, painfully average folk of Superopolis."

"Hooray for Professor Brain-Drain!" someone in the crowd began to shout. To my surprise, the chant was picked up, and little by little it spread through the crowd.

"He's just like us," asserted a woman wearing a costume made of bird feathers.

I noticed a grimace appear briefly on the Professor's face, but he quickly caught himself and gave his best grandfatherly smile.

"So true. So true." He beamed as he looked directly at me. "Never trust a smart person. In fact, I suspect we will ultimately learn that an intelligent person is somehow responsible for the disappearance of our powers. Come to think of it, I know of one such person who would have everything to gain by the elimination of all superpowers."

I got a queasy sensation in my stomach.

"After all," he continued, "who could possibly benefit more from everyone becoming ordinary than a young man named Ordinary Boy?"

CHAPTER TWENTY-SIX

Tongue-tied

It's scary to think what might have happened if my friends hadn't been there. Egged on by Professor Brain-Drain, the crowd turned angry—and ugly—fast.

"O Boy! This way!" Stench yelled as he pulled me toward him. He may not have been in full possession of his power, but he still had the size and bulk to knock away the nearest members of the mob who were pressing their way in my direction.

"Stay in between us," Tadpole hollered, suddenly at my right side. A moment later, Halogen Boy appeared on my left.

"I'll watch the back," Plasma Girl added as I felt her hand on my shoulders pushing me forward. "Let's get out of here!"

With Stench plowing a way through the crowd, and

the rest of my teammates acting as a protective cordon, we worked our way outward. But the mob still pressed closer. I was worried that even Stench wasn't going to be able to help us, when suddenly the ground began to rumble. Tremor Park was living up to its name. The shaking threw Stench to the ground just as he was about to block the Cowpoke, who was swinging a rope and rushing right toward me. I felt the rope brush against my head as I was yanked away at the very last second.

"I'll get you out of here."

I don't know how she did it, but Plasma Girl had grabbed my arm and was leading me effortlessly through the crowd even as people all around us fell to the ground in confused heaps. The earthquake seemingly had no effect on her.

"I may have lost my power," she said, answering my unspoken question, "but I still have a lifetime of experience maneuvering in a jiggly, joggly, wiggly way."

She was right. No one knew better how to ooze her way through a tricky situation then Plasma Girl. Only a moment later we reached the edge of the park, which came out at the back of the Opera House, and we came to a halt.

"You sure know how to make friends," she said between gasps of breath.

"This time it was hardly my fault," I protested. "Professor Brain-Drain is trying to make *me* the fall guy for everyone's loss of power—and they're all upset enough to believe him."

"Well, we need to get you even farther away," she said,

looking past me as her eyes widened in alarm.

I swung around and saw Tadpole, Stench, and Hal, running right toward us. But it was the mob directly behind them that got my legs moving again.

"Don't wait for us," I heard Tadpole yell as he passed us by in a blur. A second later, I had caught up with him, and all five of us were running for our lives.

I never would have thought that a bunch of out-of-shape adults could have kept chase. But I guess the opportunity to transfer their confused rage onto an innocent target gave them that extra burst of energy. They stayed pretty close for the first four or five blocks, but then, one by one, our pursuers began to fall by the wayside. Finally, after a few more blocks, I turned around and saw the last of them screech to a halt. Their faces had gone white, and without warning they turned and ran in the opposite direction.

"What's . . . that . . . all about?" Plasma Girl asked between breaths.

"They just realized they were no match for us," Tadpole boasted.

"No," I corrected him, "I don't think that was it at all. Look where we are."

"Uh-oh," Halogen Boy said softly as we all looked up at the east entry gate of the Superopolis Zoo.

"There's nothing to be afraid of." Tadpole snorted.

"They're just a bunch of dumb animals."

"Yes. Animals with powers," Plasma Girl hissed.

"She's right," I agreed. "They have powers while you all don't."

"Uh, guys?" Stench was pointing behind us.

We turned slowly and discovered we were being watched by a group of five aardvarks. None of them was over a few feet high, but the menacing expressions on their faces made all of us feel nervous. Well, almost all of us.

"HA." Tadpole let a single guffaw burst from his throat. "Look at these ridiculous creatures. What kind of stupid power do they think they can threaten us with?"

Before the words were even out of his mouth, five tongues snaked from the elongated snouts of the aardvarks. Loop after loop of wet, squishy strands wrapped around us until we found ourselves trapped in at least twenty feet each of aardvark tongue.

"Well, you were right about them having a stupid power." Stench glared at Tadpole as the aardvarks began pulling us into the zoo.

The next thing we knew we were being dragged down the main path. It should have come as no surprise who we were being taken to meet. Sure enough, only a few minutes later, the aardvarks deposited us at the feet of the velociraptor, Gore.

"Welcome to Zooperopolis." His face lit up in a razor-toothed grin. "That's what I'm calling the place now. Clever, no?"

"Yes," I admitted as the last bit of tongue unwrapped itself from me and was drawn back into the snout of the aardvark that had dragged me here. "But why have you taken us prisoner?"

"I haven't." Gore pulled back, genuinely hurt by my accusation. "I was on my way to Tremor Park to once again attempt a meeting with the mayor. So far, he's run screaming every time I've come close to making contact. Anyway, I was barely off the zoo grounds when I saw the trouble you were in. So I sent the aardvarks to drag you out of danger. I knew no one would venture into our domain, and the aardvarks' power seemed particularly useful for getting you to safety."

"See"—Tadpole stuck a finger in Stench's chest— "it *is* a useful power."

"So you're not going to eat us?" Hal asked. All our ears perked up the way they tend to do when your status as a meal is being discussed.

"Of course not," Gore replied indignantly. "Do I really seem like a monster to you?"

We glanced at his three-inch incisors, the saliva dripping from his mouth, and his razor-sharp claws.

"Oh, fine," he said with a sigh. "So I guess I do. But you should learn to judge individuals by their actions, not their appearances. Are you aware of anyone I've consumed since I've gained the power of speech?"

"Well . . . no," I admitted, "but you *are* a carnivore."

"So are you," he shot back. "Yet how many creatures have you ever hunted down and consumed on the spot."

"I caught a fish once . . ." Tadpole started to say, but shut up the instant I shot him a dirty look.

"We haven't," I said, ignoring Tadpole's fishing story.

"I'll admit that I do have a taste for meat," he said as he began to pace around. "It's a fundamental part of who I am, just as it is true for you. However, an interesting thing happened when I gained the ability to understand all other creatures. In knowing their language it was impossible for me not to know *them*."

"But you've always been aware of other creatures, haven't you?" I asked.

"Aware, yes," he agreed. "I was aware of them as a source of food. The amazing thing about speech is that through it you gain understanding. When you truly know another being, it makes it far more difficult to enjoy them as a meal."

"So what *do* you do for food?" Plasma Girl asked.

"I haven't abandoned meat completely," Gore continued, "but I can honestly say that no creature has died specifically to provide me with a meal."

"Then what *is* the main part of your diet?" I pressed.

"Why the same thing that the zoo began feeding us about a week ago," Gore explained. "In fact we're down to our very last bags."

My eyes went wide with shock as the velociraptor opened a cabinet to reveal dozens and dozens of jumbo-size bags of Dr. Telomere's Potato Chips.

CHAPTER TWENTY-SEVEN

All the Chips

The answer hit me like . . . a sack of potatoes! Everyone's powers hadn't gone away because they had *started* eating Pseudo-Chips. They had gone away because they had *stopped* eating Dr. Telomere's. And when no one wanted them anymore, they brought them all here to feed to the animals. Dr. Telomere's potato chips were the cause of everybody's superpower!

It didn't seem possible. Yet the pieces all fit. The chips went away and so did everyone's power. The animals got the chips and began developing powers. And then I remembered something from the very first time I met Professor Brain-Drain. He had served us refreshments—cookies and lemonade, but no potato chips. When Tadpole asked him about it, he replied that he never touched them. No wonder his power was gone.

My mind was awhirl. I had just stumbled on the biggest secret in the history of Superopolis! I knew I had to keep it to myself.

"Wow," I said with only a hint of the excitement I was feeling, "Dr. Telomere's! Would it be possible for me to take some of these? I ran out of my own just yesterday."

"Certainly," Gore replied without hesitation. "As we've used up this supply of potato chips, the animals have begun finding food sources of their own. Regrettably, this has included scavenging as they've roamed through your city. By doing so, they've made my eventual conversation with your mayor a more difficult one."

"I'm sorry about that," I replied. "But thank you for offering us some of what you have left, anyway."

With the help of my friends, I gathered up a dozen bags of the potato chips. Gore himself then escorted us to the front gates of the zoo and then bid us farewell.

My friends were all lively and talkative on the way home, but I found myself slipping into a funk. Now that I finally knew what caused people's powers, I also knew that in all likelihood I would never have one. I had eaten Dr. Telomere's chips my entire life. Even as a baby my parents had fed me Dr. Telomere's

Potato Chip Mush for newborns.

The realization was crushing.

When we reached my house, I instructed my friends to take two bags of chips apiece. At least they would get their powers back. I kept the remaining four for my own purposes.

"I didn't think I'd ever see a bag of Dr. Telomere's again," Halogen Boy said with a big grin on his face. "I wish there was more."

"I don't think we're seeing the last of them," I said. "But for now, let's just enjoy what we have."

Waving good-bye to my teammates, and thanking them once again for saving my behind, I turned and went inside. My parents were in the kitchen preparing dinner, but a syrupy gloom hung over everything.

"Oh, hi there, OB," my mom said, trying her best to look cheery. But the very fact that she was getting ice cubes out of the freezer to put in her iced tea spoke buckets about her mood. "How was school today?"

"It was a disaster. Every kid in my class is power-less. When we tried to play kickball, it was like they had forgotten how to walk the way they kept tripping over themselves."

"How'd my little hero do?" my dad asked as he held a match to a gas burner on our stove. As I wondered if my dad had ever done this before, a huge plume of flame whooshed up from the burner answering my question.

"AAIIEEE!" is the closest approximation of the sound he made as his eyebrows were singed off. "How do they expect people to use these things?!"

"I don't think you need to bother with cooking something tonight," I said to my dad. "I have something I think we should have instead."

Surprise spread across my parents' faces as I revealed two bags of Dr. Telomere's Potato Chips. At first there was a glimmer of joy in their eyes, and then I saw the Red Menace's power regain control.

"That's sweet of you, OB," my mom said, "but we have plenty of Pseudo-Chips on hand."

"That's right, son," Dad added as he sat down at the table next to me and picked up the bag of Dr. Telomere's. "Don't get me wrong. Dr. Telomere's makes a great product. I should know. But they just don't compare to AI's Pseudo-Chips."

"What was it like working there?" I asked as I ignored their faint protests and ripped open the bag.

"Oh, it was a huge operation—at least it used to be, anyway. On an average day, we would produce over a quarter million bags of chips—one for nearly every man, woman, and child in Superopolis."

"People used to love these chips," I stated as I emptied the bag into the big chip bowl in the center of our table. "What do you suppose it was about them that folks liked so much?"

"That's easy," my dad said. "It was the crunch! And that's where your old man came in," he added as he elbowed me.

"It's true," my mom added. "Your father heated the fryers at Dr. Telomere's to exactly the right temperature. That's how they were able to achieve that distinctive, delicious crunch."

She sat down at the table and I noticed both her and my father staring at the bowl of Dr. Telomere's potato chips.

"I'll bet they have a far better crunch than those Pseudo-Chips could ever have," I said nonchalantly as I nudged the bowl in their direction.

Mom and Dad stared at the golden, perfectly fried little beauties. Each one was its own unique creation—no two alike. Simultaneously, my parents reached for a chip. I watched with only a hint of trepidation as they each brought one to their mouths. The sound of a crunch on either side of me was like a symphony.

"I-I had forgotten how good these are," my mother said with confusion lining her face. "But how could I have forgotten?"

"It wasn't you," I said with more relief than I had ever felt before. "It was the Red Menace. He's brainwashed everyone into thinking that Pseudo-Chips are better."

"But they taste awful," my father said as he finally broke free of the Red Menace's control over him. He shoved three real potato chips into his mouth at one time. "Nothing compares to Dr. Telomere's."

My parents were back to their old selves. The straitjacket of worry that had gripped me all week was gone as Mom, Dad, and I sat around the kitchen table, talking and laughing and eating chips. I ate sparingly, knowing that I needed to let my parents get the most from them.

While they ate, I glanced once again at the cartoon potato chip on the bag's logo. My dad said that Dr. Telomere was a marketing device, but what about the Ambrose Telomere from the logbook of the S.S. *Befuddlement*?

As soon as I went up to my room, I pulled out my trusty copy of the *Li'l Hero's Handbook*. I flipped first to the Ds, where I saw the entry for the factory itself. But then I paged all the way back to the Ts. My eyes went

NAME: Telomere, Dr. Ambrose. **POWER:** Time will always tell. **LIMITATIONS:** Only those we place on ourselves. **CAREER:** Too many to list. **CLASSIFICATION:** You're invited to see. Your password is FREE.

wide as I found the following entry:

Who *was* Ambrose Telomere? It seemed I was being offered an invitation to find out—and I had no intention of passing it up.

CHAPTER TWENTY-EIGHT

The Factory

This was one mission I needed to handle on my own, so at the end of class on Tuesday I slipped away before any of my friends noticed. I walked the few blocks to my house and continued past it heading west. I soon came to a vast stretch of potato fields that ran to the north and south of me as far as I could see.

Directly ahead of me across the fields was the Dr. Telomere's Potato Chip Factory. It would be a long walk out of my way to go up to the road that led to the factory, so instead I struck out in a direct route across the fields. As I hiked over the rich-looking soil, I saw that there was a bumper crop of spuds waiting to be harvested.

Upon reaching the end of the field, I stepped onto a large, empty parking lot. With no chips being made, the factory was deserted. Besides, the Red Menace had lured away any remaining employees for his Pseudo-Chip operation.

I headed toward the entrance and was surprised to find the main door unlocked. I let myself in to a vast, airy lobby. Hanging from the ceiling nearly fifty feet above my head was an enormous mobile made of dozens and dozens of giant, floating potato chips. I recognized it immediately as the work of the famous artist Crispo—who had only recently been revealed to be Professor Brain-Drain's alter ego. The massive chips swayed eerily in the otherwise silent space.

"Hellooo," I called out. "Is anybody here?"

There was no reply, so I made my way toward a main corridor, assuming it would lead me into the factory. When I was only a few yards away from the hallway, a barrier came plummeting down with a loud, echoing bang and blocked the entrance. I spun around, wondering how I was going to get into the factory when I spotted a single unmarked door at the far end of the lobby. As I made my way toward it, I realized there was a small sign on the door: THIS WAY! Funny thing, I could swear that a minute earlier it hadn't been there.

I went through the door and found myself in a long,

246

tunnel-like passage. I began following it. At first the walls of the corridor were bare. But then I came to a stretch that was decorated with framed art. The first piece was a portrait of the Dr. Telomere advertising character. It was that familiar image of a potato chip wearing a derby, a bow tie, and pince-nez. The next portrait down was also of Dr. Telomere. I recognized it as the version of the character that had appeared on the bags when I was in kindergarten. It looked a lot like the current incarnation but with some subtle differences.

As I continued, the portraits became more and more old-fashioned. I was clearly following a backward progression of the visual look of the Dr. Telomere character. What had first been pictures of a cartoon potato chip became more realistic looking as I moved along. By the fifth portrait the potato chip was fully clothed. By the eighth, it had hair, and two pictures farther it showed a potato chip with a trim beard. From there the character began to get increasingly more human looking. By the time I reached the end of the line of portraits I was staring up at a painting of a man who looked just like the person pictured in the *Li'l Hero's Handbook* under the entry for Dr. Ambrose Telomere. He still wore a derby, the bow tie, and the glasses.

I was so fascinated by the portrait gallery, it took me a moment to notice that the corridor had come to a dead end. There wasn't even a door—just a screen with a keypad. I pushed one of the buttons and the screen lit up.

PASSWORD, PLEASE, it said in glowing white letters. I hesitated for only a moment then punched in the letters F-R-E-E. No sooner had I done so then the wall slid away. A brilliant white light flooded over me.

I stepped out into an open area filled with the most enormous equipment you could imagine, all sitting somberly quiet. I was in the chip-making heart of the factory.

My mouth dropped open. I had wanted to see this ever since I was old enough to know what my father did for a living. He had described it numerous times, but he always refused my pleas to see it. He insisted that it was too dangerous for a child. Then, without warning, the factory burst into life, and it became obvious why he had thought so.

A huge, dump truck–size bin, hanging from enormous cables, lurched forward until it hovered above a gigantic, clear glass hopper. The bottom of the bin suddenly dropped open, and potatoes rained into the hopper. Inside, I watched them getting a bath as scrubbers and brushes and a continuous shower of water removed any dirt that remained on them. From there, the squeaky-clean potatoes emerged and began rumbling along a conveyor belt. It carried them toward an enormous clear drum that resembled a cement mixer. There, I could see the potatoes being tossed and turned as they rubbed up against a sandpaperlike surface that bit by bit was scuffing away their skins. At the narrow base of the spinning device, peeled potatoes were emerging and continuing on their path down the conveyor belt.

The next step was the slicer. This was a nasty-looking implement that was mostly hidden from view. Whole potatoes tumbled into it, but paper thin slices came out below. At this point, as if the potatoes hadn't suffered enough abuse, the slices dropped directly into a river of bubbling oil that coursed its way along a narrow channel. I wondered how it was being heated now that my father didn't work here any longer.

I followed the sizzling trail as it rolled ahead, the potato slices getting evermore golden as they sailed along in it. Just as the chips were reaching their perfect color, mechanical arms with baskets for hands began dipping into the superhot oil, removing the chips in batches. From there the river of grease circled back to where it had begun and where more potato slices plunged into it.

Meanwhile, the finished chips were being deposited onto yet another conveyor belt. This one shook them gently, getting rid of any excess oil. Finally, the chips passed under a gentle snowfall of salt before dropping into a large funnel-shaped bin.

As I stood right in front of the bin, a parade of empty potato chip bags passed beneath it. One by one, each bag was filled to the top, then sealed.

The smell was amazing! I couldn't resist reaching for one of the bags. As I did, a voice surprised me from behind.

"Please do help yourself!"

I swung around to find myself facing a very old man with a neat goatee. He wore a bow tie, pince-nez, and a derby.

"Dr. Telomere?" I ventured.

"Of course," he replied. "I've been expecting you."

CHAPTER TWENTY-NINE

Dr. Telomere

"How . . . who . . . what?" was all I could get to come out of my mouth.

"My name is on the bag," he replied as he grabbed one of the packages of chips from the assembly line. "But my picture has changed so much over the years that I doubt anyone would recognize me anymore. That's how I'm able to move about this factory without even my employees knowing who I really am. At least back when I still *had* employees." He chuckled. "The hall you entered through containing my portrait gallery isn't seen by anyone I don't *want* to have see it."

"You *must* be Dr. Telomere," I agreed. "You're included in the *Li'l Hero's Handbook*, and it's never been wrong."

"Ahhh!" His face lit up as I held up my copy. "So you find that book handy, do you?"

"It's fantastic." I beamed. "It even told me how to find you."

"Yes"—he smiled—"I did include that invitation when I had the book printed."

"YOU created the *Li'l Hero's Handbook*?" I said in amazement. "There's no mention of an author or publisher anywhere inside. That was the first mystery I noticed about the book when I found it on sale at the Mighty Mart a few years ago."

"Yes, it was my one and only publishing venture." He nodded.

"You must have sold thousands of them," I gushed. "And I'll bet hundreds of other people have found their way here to meet you before me."

"One would think." Dr. Telomere nodded. "I had displays of the handbook set up in every place in town that sold my potato chips."

"I remember the display," I interrupted. "It said 'All the Secrets of the Universe Explained!' Who could have resisted that?"

"Apparently, everyone." He shrugged. "Everyone, that is, except you."

"What?!" I exclaimed.

"It's true," he said. "I sold only a single copy—the very one you bought. It confirmed two things I had always suspected. One was that no one should ever go into publishing if they want to make money."

"What was the other thing?" I asked.

"That the people of Superopolis are almost totally lacking in curiosity."

"I can confirm that one," I admitted sadly. "Even at my school they seem to frown on questions. Lately I've been asking about the early years of Superopolis's history, but nobody else seems to care. With my friends, though, I was able to discover that the story involves the S.S. *Befuddlement*."

"You are absolutely correct," Dr. Telomere said with a smile. "And if you would like, it is a story I would be happy to tell you."

"I'm dying to know," I said eagerly.

"You are indeed curious." He chuckled approvingly. "Well, the story begins, as you have guessed, aboard the misnamed research vessel the S.S. *Befuddlement*. I say misnamed because the ship was in fact a floating library of scientific study, and its passengers were anything but befuddled. The name was purposely chosen to deflect attention. You see, the ship carried the greatest assemblage of scientists ever brought together in one place."

"What kind of scientists?" I asked.

"Oh, all kinds," he replied. "There were zoologists who had accumulated a remarkable collection of animal species below the decks. The ship had astronomers who charted the night skies and explored the mysteries of the cosmos. Geologists on board had made discoveries about the very origins of the Earth itself. And there was even a botanist who had investigated plant species from around the world in an attempt to breed the hardiest varieties of the most useful crops. The ship was a wonder of science, and it was all thanks to the financial support of the seventeenth Lord Pincushion."

I perked up in surprise at the familiar name.

"No, not the one you know today," Dr. Telomere pointed out. "His ancestor. He was a patron of the sciences and used his considerable wealth to support their study. For many years the *Befuddlement* sailed the globe. It was on the return from one such trip, with the ship's hold filled with specimens, that they sailed into a harbor to unload. The botanist was particularly eager to empty the holds and be back to sea quickly. You see, the ship's next scientific journey was to a little-known

255

dot in the ocean called Cow Pie Island."

"Cow Pie Island?"

"Yes," Dr. Telomere confirmed. "And that's exactly what it looked like. A lump of cow poop sitting in the middle of the ocean."

I wrinkled my nose at the description.

"But there was something special about this island. Only one thing was said to grow on it—the hardiest variety of potatoes known on the planet—the legendary Cow Pie Golds."

"Cow Pie Golds?" I repeated skeptically.

"That's really what they were called," he insisted. "You'll just have to trust me on this one. Anyway, the crew had barely begun unloading their cargo of plants and animals when word somehow got out to the local population about the ship's next destination. Of course they completely misunderstood the purpose of the trip. They assumed the ship was on its way to an island rich in deposits of real gold.

"I see where it would be an easy mistake to make," I said.

"Yes, I agree," admitted Dr. Telomere. "But some people had mistaken the cow pie part, as well. A number of them assumed that the island was home to cows that baked particularly delicious desserts."

"I guess there have always been people who aren't

very bright," I shrugged.

"Quite right," he said with a sigh. "And no small number of them swarmed aboard the boat. Finally, Lord Pincushion had to have the ship set out to sea in order to keep it from being capsized. Despite those efforts, over a thousand unwanted passengers had managed to get aboard. Pincushion didn't want to let them stay on the ship, but he also couldn't go back to shore where even more people were waiting for a chance to get on board.

"When he found out *why* they had swarmed his ship, he was outraged. To teach them a lesson he decided to actually take them to Cow Pie Island. There he set them to work harvesting a huge crop of the Cow Pie Golds to not only fill the ship's hold and sustain the crew and livestock but also to feed the enormous number of unwanted passengers who were now exhausted, homesick, and feeling nearly as foolish as they actually were.

"With the passengers now chastised, the *Befuddlement* set sail for the port it had come from. But then disaster struck. A storm came out of nowhere. For nearly three days the ship was tossed and battered and blown so far off course that not even the captain could plot their location. Finally, on the fourth day, the ship was washed onto a rocky outcropping of land where an

257

enormous hole was ripped into its side. The passengers all swarmed ashore and found themselves on a lush beautiful plain that stretched toward the tallest mountains any of them had ever seen."

"The Carbunkle Mountains."

"Yes"—he nodded—"and the land—as you've probably guessed—was unoccupied. The topography explained why. The Carbunkle Mountains looped around to the north and the south, and on both sides they ran into the ocean. This created a plain ten miles long, by five miles wide with unpassable mountains on three sides and an inhospitable ocean as the remaining barrier—the Ornery Ocean they named it for just that reason."

"And that's how Superopolis was settled?" I said. "Every resident of Superopolis is descended from someone aboard that ship?"

"Most of them," he said. "The earthquakes and frequent eruptions were a bit unsettling at first, but people quickly got used to them. The large assortment of animals and plant species aboard the ship were quickly incorporated into the ecosystem as well. And the Cow Pie Golds thrived in the rich and fertile soil, becoming the new community's primary source of food."

"The botanist must have been overjoyed," I said

looking him directly in the eye.

"He most certainly was," Dr. Telomere responded without blinking. A corner of his mouth lifted slightly in amusement. "It became his life's work."

"It became *your* life's work, you mean," I contended. "I found your name in the logbook of the S.S. *Befuddlement*. Just exactly how old are you, Dr. Telomere?"

"Very good, son." He began to laugh heartily. "You almost caught me as I left the ship the other day. I was there returning its long-absent logbook precisely so you could find it. In the process, you've discovered my power as well. So I guess it's only fair to answer your question honestly. I am," he announced, "just over two hundred and seventy-three years old."

CHAPTER THIRTY

A Powerful Secret

"You're immortal," I said matter-of-factly.

"Well, I wouldn't say that," Dr. Telomere replied. "After all, you don't really know if you're immortal until you've lived forever—and that will be a difficult thing to ever prove. But I certainly have lived long beyond my allotted span, and I show no signs of slowing down anytime soon."

"And you've been making potato chips this entire time?"

"Almost from the minute we landed." He laughed. "At first, the Cow Pie Golds were the only source of food we had. They were also the quickest to grow. The other plant specimens I had on board the ship took much longer to expand into functioning crops."

"What about superpowers?" I added. "When did *they* start to appear?"

261

"Shortly after we harvested our first potato crop," he answered. "The shock was staggering. People had no idea what was happening and were terrified at first. But they quickly got over it and adapted to their newfound abilities as if they'd had them their entire lives. I was fascinated—not only by what I was witnessing but also by the realization that I was apparently unaffected."

"So when *did* you discover your power?" I asked.

"Oh, not for a very long time," he replied. "In fact, it was many decades after everyone else had begun showing their superabilities. For the longest time I assumed that I had no power of any kind. After all, mine doesn't reveal itself in any flashy way other than by the passage of time. It wasn't until after all those who I had arrived on the island with were gone that I finally realized the truth."

"So a person can show no sign at all, yet still have a superpower?" I asked far too eagerly. Dr. Telomere picked up on it instantly.

"Absolutely." He smiled kindly. "I'm not certain what your power is, my boy, but I would be very surprised indeed if you did not possess one."

My face lit up with optimism at these words. It wasn't a guarantee, but it was the closest I had ever gotten to someone telling me I might not be so different after all. Then a curious thought struck me—did I want to be just like everyone else? Dr. Telomere caught the change of expression on my face.

"Getting something that you've always thought you've wanted doesn't necessarily mean things will work out the way you expect."

"You're right," I admitted. "I thought that if I could discover what causes everybody's power, it might help me discover mine. But even knowing that secret may not tell me anything about myself."

"It may not," Dr. Telomere agreed. "But what *have* you figured out about the source of power?"

"Well, at first I thought that the Red Menace had developed potato chips that took away people's powers," I explained, "but then I realized that it didn't provide any kind of an answer as to where powers came from to begin with."

"That's correct." He nodded.

"So then, when my friends and I discovered the giant prodigium meteorite buried beneath your water tower, it only seemed natural that it had to be having *some* kind of an effect."

"So you concluded that radiation from the meteorite had caused everything," Dr. Telomere hinted. "Very clever."

"Only for a moment," I replied. "Upon discovering the meteorite, I also discovered Professor Brain-Drain. He, too, believed it was the radiation's effect on the water supply that was the cause. But the Professor himself proved otherwise by revealing that he, also, is without a power."

"You don't say?" Dr. Telomere nodded. "I've suspected that something wasn't right with him. With the exception of his spectacular scheme a couple weeks ago, he's been unusually quiet these past ten years. Where did your investigation lead you next?"

"Here, of course," I answered. "It's the potatoes, isn't it?"

He merely stood there smiling at me with a glimmer in his eyes.

"If there's one thing I've determined with certainty," I pressed ahead, "it's that *you* know the answer and can tell me if I'm right or wrong."

Dr. Telomere didn't say a word. At first I thought he was going to just ignore my accusation, but then he started chuckling.

"You're right, my boy—and yet still wrong. The prodigium does indeed irradiate the water supply—and in this particular case the water I store in the tower atop Crater Hill. I use that water to irrigate the vast fields that grow my potatoes. But the potatoes themselves do nothing—until the final step."

He glanced away, his eyes darting around to the assembly-line process taking place all around us—the potatoes being peeled and sliced, the slices dropping into the oil. . . .

"It's the oil!" I blurted out, more as a statement than a question. "Or more precisely, the heat! Frying the potatoes causes the change. It's the potato *chips*, not the potatoes themselves that are the cause!"

"Bingo!" Dr. Telomere exclaimed. "The water subtly alters the makeup of the Cow Pie Golds, and the heat causes a molecular change in them. In the process, a previously unknown chemical—which I've dubbed superose—is produced. It's the superose that causes powers to develop. I discovered the unusual side effect of my chips totally by accident after I began selling them. It took years of additional experimenting before I figured out the entire chain of events that led to this unique result. You, lad, figured it out in mere days."

"The clues were all there." I blushed.

"Yes. The clues are all there for everyone"—he nodded solemnly—"but other than me, only you put them all together and came up with the answer."

"Why has no one else ever tried?" I asked perplexed. "Why wouldn't people want to know?"

"People in general are remarkably incurious, and the citizens of Superopolis are particularly so," he replied. "I suppose it makes life easier not to question anything around them. Unfortunately, that also makes them less intelligent. After all, you can't become smarter if you have no interest in learning the answers to questions."

"Not everyone lacks curiosity," I reminded him.

"Very true," he agreed. "All of the Lords Pincushion have been intelligent individuals, and the current one assembled an entire team of such heroes."

"The League of Goodness!" I confirmed. "But I was thinking of somebody else, actually—Professor Brain-Drain."

"Ah, yes," Dr. Telomere said with all seriousness. "He's a perfect example of what can happen when knowledge is put toward evil purposes. There probably hasn't been a more curious, and intelligent, citizen of Superopolis—at least until I started following your progress, my boy."

"My progress?" I said, taken aback. "But why? How long could you possibly have known about me?"

"Oh, since shortly after you were born," he admitted. "It always catches my attention when I hear of children who don't show any outward signs of a power," he explained. "As you're probably aware, people's powers tend to fall into two distinct categories: abilities and deformities."

"Deformities?!" I said, lurching back.

"Well, that was the term I used at first. When people sprout an extra limb or their hair turns into yarn . . ."

"Or their head looks like a watermelon . . ." I added.

"Exactly," he agreed. "I used the word strictly as a scientific categorization, but the people who had these various . . . abnormalities . . . took offense at the term."

"I'm hardly surprised," I said.

"Besides, they loved their newfound 'uniqueness,'" he said with a shrug. "Eventually the term fell out of favor."

"And the second group . . . ?"

"The other classification covered those individuals who looked perfectly normal but possessed abilities that ranged from the spectacular to the less than useless."

"I know both kinds," I admitted.

Dr. Telomere chuckled. "Well, needless to say, it was among this second group where I would occasionally hear about some newborn who didn't appear to have a power. I would always first make sure that he or she had been fed a regular diet of my Potato Chip Mush baby food, and then continue to observe the situation discreetly. In all cases, it only took a little time to determine the child's power.

The one and only exception has been you."

"You've been watching me all this time?" I said in disbelief.

"Not directly watching you, no." He shook his head. "But I found a particularly effective way of always getting information about your progress."

"My father," I said, without even having to think about it.

"Exactly!" he confirmed. "By hiring Thermo to work here I not only was able to hear about your progress on a daily basis but also got an incredibly effective and cost-efficient method of heating my fryers. It was quite a blow to me in both respects when he chose to leave and pursue his superhero career once again. My energy bills skyrocketed."

"And now you have a business that has ceased completely because of the Amazing Indestructo and the Red Menace."

"Mostly because of the Red Menace," Dr. Telomere agreed. "Even with all his advertising, the Amazing Indestructo would never have been able to convince the populace to switch over to those baked scraps of preformed paste that he's producing."

"But you know exactly how to return everyone's power," I blurted out. "You just have to let people know."

"Do I?" he replied cryptically. "Do you think people

really want to know that something they take such pride in is merely the side effect of their diets?"

"No," I grudgingly admitted, thinking back on my own experience at the hands of a room of hostile fifth graders. "But then how do things get returned to the way they were?"

"Maybe they don't," he said seriously. "For more than two centuries I've let a situation persist that maybe should never have happened at all. Maybe this is an experiment that has finally reached its conclusion. Would you be so upset if everyone were to remain . . . ordinary?"

I stood there silently asking myself that very question. How *would* I feel if everyone was left in the same position as me?

"It's not just a theoretical question, my boy," Dr. Telomere went on as I remained in silent thought. "You see, I'm leaving the decision to you."

CHAPTER THIRTY-ONE

Decisions, Decisions

The decision was mine.

Those were the words that Dr. Telomere had left me with. As I tossed and turned in my bed that night, they echoed through my brain like a fateful decree. I feared the weight of responsibility hanging over me might crush me.

What was I to do? At last I had a power—possibly the most awesome anyone had ever possessed. I had the power over every resident of Superopolis to either return their abilities to them—or not. If I did so, they would once again have the special gifts they believed formed the core of who they were. Or I could do nothing, and leave everyone in the same position as me.

I'd be lying if I said I wasn't tempted to do just

that. My entire life had been a nonstop reminder that I was different. The thought that I had the ability to change all that coursed through me with a fiery rush. Why shouldn't I put an end to an unnatural system that gave some an unfair advantage over others? Why *shouldn't* everyone be equal?

But I already knew the answer to that question. The Red Menace wanted to make everyone equal, too—with no more personality or individuality than a stack of Amazing Indestructo Pseudo-Chips. I didn't need to hear it coming from a wannabe tyrant to know that such a goal was utterly evil. People are always going to be different. Some will be more talented artists than others, while some will be better athletes. There will be those who get the looks but not the brains, while others get the brains and not the looks. Some lucky few will get both; some will get neither.

And none of these things were guarantees of happiness. The Amazing Indestructo appeared to have everything. Yet I had come to realize he wasn't a very happy person. I wouldn't have traded places with him for anything in the world.

Then there were the practical aspects of the decision. If everyone was left powerless, it would be as good as letting the Red Menace win. It was becoming clear to me that he must also know the secret of the potato chips. Why else would he have used his power to switch everybody over to the Pseudo-Chips? But how had he discovered the truth while locked away for fifty years? That was another mystery I needed to solve.

Professor Brain-Drain was also a major concern. Unless I found a way to stop him, he would most likely be the next mayor of Superopolis. Unlike the ineffectual and harmless Mayor Whitewash, Professor Brain-Drain could do some serious damage if he were to win. And if everyone remained powerless, he almost certainly *was* going to win.

What would a true hero do? I asked myself.

The answer was clear. Dr. Telomere's potato chips would have to be brought back, and AI's Pseudo-Chips would have to go. Everyone would regain their powers while I would continue to have no power at all. But I *would* have the hope that Dr. Telomere had left me with—that I just might have a power that simply hadn't revealed itself yet.

With the decision made, my anxiety was replaced with exhaustion and I finally drifted off to sleep. The question of *how* I was going to accomplish this would just have to wait.

* * *

The next morning I woke to the sound of voices drifting up from our living room. Getting out of bed I pulled on my jeans and a clean white T-shirt and made my way downstairs. There I found an emergency meeting of the New New Crusaders in full swing. Even Stench's mom, Chrysanthemum, was there, making for a complete reunion of the original New Crusaders. They were in the midst of a heated discussion.

"The problem is that we've all lost our powers," Windbag was blustering. "I don't know why you keep going on about AI's chips."

"We think that AI's chips are sapping our powers," my dad was insisting.

"Thermo is right," my mom said in support. "As soon as we all started eating those chips, our powers vanished."

As I stood there, listening to their discussion, I had an idea. I had assumed that it was going to be necessary to reveal the power of Dr. Telomere's chips to everyone in Superopolis in order to foil the Red Menace's plans. But now I was getting another idea—one that would allow the secret of the chips to remain under wraps.

"It's true," I said loudly enough for them to all turn and notice me. "My friends and I discovered

that Comrade Crunch is really a paroled super-villain named the Red Menace. He admitted right to our faces that he would use the chips to make everyone in Superopolis equal—equally powerless. He obviously used all his years in prison developing a potato chip that would block everyone's powers."

"But Pseudo-Chips are so good," Windbag whined in despair. "They're all I eat anymore."

"That's the truth." Chrysanthemum rolled her eyes in annoyance.

"They're lighter and crispier than any other chips," the Levitator insisted.

"They're the primary cause of you all losing your endorsement deal with Maximizer Snack Cakes," I pointed out.

"Maximizer *Brand* Snack Cakes," my dad corrected me.

"Wait here," I said as I bolted into the kitchen and grabbed another of the bags of Dr. Telomere's chips that I had brought with me from the zoo. I returned to the living room, bringing a chip bowl with me as well.

"You've all been brainwashed to forget what really good potato chips taste like," I said as I ripped open the bag and poured half the chips into the bowl. "Taste these and tell me if you honestly believe Pseudo-Chips even come close."

Reluctantly our four guests reached for a chip as my mom and dad watched. The proud looks on their faces were all I needed to know that my decision last night had been the right one. And the look of pleasant surprise on the face of each New New Crusader told me that I had broken the spell the Red Menace had had over them.

"You're right, OB." The Big Bouncer blinked a few times as if he were clearing his head. "These are fantastic. How could I ever have thought AI's chips were better than these?"

"It wasn't your fault," I explained. "It was the Red Menace. But now it's up to all of you to let everybody once again taste the superiority of Dr. Telomere's chips."

"But how?" My dad shrugged. "The factory is closed. Dr. Telomere's is out of business."

"You know how the factory runs," I reminded him. "You may not have your power back yet, but with the help of the New New Crusaders you can still get production up and running again. When people taste Dr. Telomere's chips again, that will be it for the Pseudo-Chips. And the New New Crusaders will be the team that made it all happen."

"The boy's a genius," my dad said as he clamped his hands down on my shoulders. A warm glow spread throughout me—literally. There was a faint heat coming from my father's hands.

CHAPTER THIRTY-TWO

That's the Ticket!

I was confident that my father's team would soon have Dr. Telomere's fully up and running. But how was I going to get the entire city to switch chips? Not only that, how was I going to prevent Professor Brain-Drain from being elected mayor? There had to be some way to derail his bid for the office.

"Miss Marble?" I raised my hand, interrupting her as she explained how important it is for a politician to know his own flaws so he can accuse his opponent of the same things first. "What exactly are the qualifications for being able to run for mayor?"

"Other than breathing?" she asked. "Well, you have to have an oversize ego. And tons of money is helpful, too."

"But what about legal requirements?" I pressed.

"Legal?" she said, partly to herself. "Well, you have to be at least old enough to vote. Oh, yeah, and you can't ever have been convicted of a crime. That usually happens *after* you've been in office."

None of this was of any use. Professor Brain-Drain was certainly old enough, and he had *said* he'd never been convicted of a crime—as hard as that was for me to believe. Then it hit me! Professor Brain-Drain himself admitted he had tried draining the Red Menace's brain ten years ago. How else could he have done that unless he was in prison, too? Before I made that kind of an accusation, though, I was going to need proof.

I was so distracted by this idea that it caught me by surprise when Tadpole asked for permission to get up and make a speech. What was he doing? We hadn't planned for him to speak.

"Fellow classmates," he began solemnly, "we have a crucial decision to make. With our powers gone, it's more important than ever to cast our votes wisely. That's why you need to vote for the candidates who are clearly smarter."

Uh-oh. If there was one thing I had learned from Miss Marble, it was that nobody buys into the idea that a smart candidate is a better choice when it comes to elections.

"Just three weeks ago, when he had us prisoner in

his lair atop the Vertigo Building, Professor Brain-Drain himself attempted to drain away the intelligence of all three of our top candidates," Tadpole continued as if this proved our superiority. "Can our opponents say likewise? In a world of no powers, smarts matter."

"Ha! Their side has already given up on getting our powers back," Cannonball accused, sensing the easy opening that Tadpole had just given him. "But if you vote for me and Melonhead, we promise to return everybody's powers right after we're elected."

"Right," snorted Tadpole as he scrambled to recover from his error. "Like you have the ability to give or take away everyone's powers. That's ridiculous!"

Tadpole was right, of course, but I knew a lot of my classmates were taking what Cannonball said seriously. They really believed him. I knew I had to act.

"Cannonball claims he can bring back your powers if you vote for him." I quickly rose to address the class. "That's a lie, of course. But I'll make you a different promise. Our side will solve this problem and bring back everyone's powers *before* the election."

The looks of surprise on my classmates' faces were nothing compared to my teammates', who gaped at me like I was crazy.

"If we fail, you should all vote for Cannonball and his puppet, Melonhead," I announced as Melonhead turned around and glared at me. "But if we succeed," I added after a suitable pause, "I expect all of your votes to be cast for us."

The final bell rang at that moment and my teammates erupted in a frenzy of frustration.

"Are you crazy?!" shouted Tadpole. "How are we going to do that?!"

"Tadpole's right," agreed Stench. "If we can't deliver on that promise, we're sunk!"

"Nice work, O Boy! You've just won us the election!" Cannonball guffawed as he walked past us.

"Way to go," the Quake added as she "accidentally" bumped into me.

Tadpole couldn't restrain himself and began needling Cannonball. It wasn't long before the two competing political parties were in a full-scale clash. I could see Miss Marble was completely flustered by her inability to put a stop to it, and I decided to use the commotion as my opportunity to slip away from my friends.

I knew that I *could* return everyone's powers. But to do so, I had to convince people go back to Dr. Telomere's chips. I also had to find proof of Professor Brain-Drain's jail time. Luckily, the solutions to both problems could be found at the same place. I slipped away from the school playground and headed for downtown. It was time to pay a visit to city hall.

When I got there, I was in such a hurry that I almost didn't notice the dejected group of heroes sulking on the park benches in front of the building. It was a sad assemblage of seven members of the League of Ultimate Goodness. At first I thought they all looked depressed because Major Bummer was sitting with them, but then I realized he had lost his power to spread doom and gloom. This despair was genuine.

"Well, hello thar, Ordinary Boy," Whistlin' Dixie said, trying to sound cheerful. "What brings ya down here to city hall?"

"I'm just here on an errand," I said. "Why are all of you here?"

"We came down to file for unemployment bene-fits," said the Crimson Creampuff. "But there's nobody in the office."

"What happened to your jobs?" I asked.

"AI, he-a laid us off," Spaghetti Man admitted.

"Aaarrgh, it's true," confirmed Captain Blowhole. "The scurvy dog said he couldn't afford to pay us while he was out of commission."

"Why?" I said. "He lost his power, not his fortune."

"It's not the money," grumped Major Bummer. "It's because with him powerless, he's no better than any of us."

"He doesn't want to take a chance on anyone

NAME: Cap'n Blowhole. **POWER:** The ability to shoot water from the top of his head. **LIMITATIONS:** Has difficulty holding onto hats. **CAREER:** After one too many harpoon incidents, the Cap'n, for his own safety, accepted an offer to join the League of Ultimate Goodness. **CLASSIFICATION:** Always a bit soggy.

showing him up," added the Human Compass.

"He's pathetic," I said, my anger growing. And then I got an idea.

"Say, how would all of you like to get back at AI?"

"Vhat is it, darling?" asked Mannequin. "I'm feeling vonderfully vindictive at zee moment."

"My dad and his team are getting Dr. Telomere's up and running even as we speak," I explained. "If they can get real potato chips out to the public, it might just sink AI's Pseudo-Chip business. I know they'd welcome the help of anyone who's working against the Amazing Indestructo."

"It would serve that egotistical basket case right," mused Major Bummer as he glanced at his teammates. No one disagreed.

"Pardner, ya got yerself a deal," Dixie said, tipping her rhinestone hat.

As the former LUGs headed off on their new mission, I climbed the steps to city hall. Like the league had said, the place was deserted. It was as if the city employees had already given up any hope of Mayor Whitewash retaining his job. I had two errands to run, though, so I ignored the silence and followed the signs for the hall of public records.

I found it quickly, but it, too, was empty. Glancing around, I slipped behind the front desk and headed straight for the files labeled POLICE RECORDS. I pulled open the drawer containing the Ps and began to riffle through them. Sure enough, I found a sliver-thin file with the Professor's name on it. I opened it up to reveal a single piece of paper.

Bingo! I had found what I needed. Not only did I know how to put an end to Professor Brain-Drain's political career but also how I could steer everyone away from AI's Pseudo-Chips. All I needed was the cooperation of Mayor Whitewash—as well as the item I had been carrying in my book bag! Uncinching it, I reached in and retrieved my last bag of Dr. Telomere's Potato Chips. Now, I only had to get the mayor to try the chips. When his power returned, he would just assume it was from *not* eating the Pseudo-Chips, and then he could begin convincing everyone else.

I found the mayor's office and came to a stop outside the ornate door that bore his name on a thick brass plate. I paused for only a moment as I took a deep breath and then entered.

The large, lavish room was as empty as the rest of city hall—including the mayor's enormous desk. And then I noticed that the desk chair was turned away from the door, and a thick shock of white hair was poking over the top of it.

"Mayor Whitewash," I blurted out in excitement as I held up the bag of Dr. Telomere's chips, "I know how to help you win the election."

"Is that so?" came a voice that turned my blood cold.

I watched in dismay as the chair spun around to reveal none other than the Red Menace himself.

CHAPTER THIRTY-THREE

The Odd Couple

I slowly backed toward the door as the Red Menace began to laugh at me. And then he spotted the bag of Dr. Telomere's chips in my hand and the laughing stopped cold. It was all the confirmation I needed that he was fully aware of their power.

"Where did you get those?" he demanded.

"I found them at the zoo," I replied.

"Yes, that would explain the superpowered animals," he said, "but it doesn't explain how *you* came to know about the benefits of these chips."

"The answer is there for anyone who wants to see it," I stated.

"Answers are often right in front of our faces," he said with a sneer as he got up stiffly and moved from behind the desk. "Yet most people prefer not to see them. They want only simple answers to life's questions—regardless of whether they're correct. But not you, apparently."

"A wrong answer is no answer at all," I said, deciding to stand my ground as he approached.

"That's just the kind of individualistic thinking that I will soon eliminate completely," he threatened. "I've already spread equality to the entire population, and now it requires only my strong hand to lead them to a brilliant new future. Don't you agree?"

"Yes . . . I mean *no*!" I said forcing myself to break the grip of his power as he used it on me at full strength. "I notice you've kept your own power functioning. Why not make yourself as equal as everyone else?"

"If only I could." He feigned exhaustion. "Yet I'm willing to make that sacrifice, as any selfless leader would."

"Real leaders at least get themselves elected," I pointed out.

"Oh, you mean politicians," the Red Menace replied with a sinister laugh. "Their positions will soon be abolished."

"Abolished?"

"Certainly. This will become an office for all the people—" he started to say as he waved his hand to indicate the space we were in.

"I doubt they'll all fit," I interrupted.

"—but I'll occupy it on their behalf," he concluded. "That's why I'm here, in fact. To check out my future home."

"What have you done with Mayor Whitewash," I demanded.

"Nothing," he stated. "I would never cause harm to my own son."

"Your *son*?" I said, unable to hide my shock.

"Of course," he said matter-of-factly. "Surely you noticed the similarity of our powers. Sadly, Whitewash has only a watered-down version of my ability. While I can compel people to *do* whatever I tell them, he can merely convince them to *believe* the things he tells them. Believing is not the same thing as doing, you have to admit."

"Lots of people believe they'll become million-aires," I agreed, "but few actually do."

"Exactly." He nodded. "Still, it's certainly a useful power for a politician."

"Except that you've taken it away from him. And without it, he has no chance of winning."

"Yes, that's true," the Red Menace admitted. "In fact, I made certain he lost his power before everyone else. Not that anyone was going to be able to counteract my commands, but if anybody could come close, it would have been him, as you yourself surmised. No matter. His office is about to become irrelevant anyway."

"Really?" I asked. "Are you unaware that you've made it possible for Professor Brain-Drain to become mayor? That can't be part of your plan."

"Ha! Professor Brain-Drain is no threat to me," he scoffed. "Brain-Drain is powerless. I robbed him of his ability ten years ago."

"But you were in prison," I pointed out.

"And so was he," the Red Menace responded, confirming the same information I had just uncovered in the record room. "I was serving a sentence of one thousand six hundred and thirty-six years in solitary confinement. Because of my power, I was allowed to see no one out of fear that I might bend him or her to my will."

"Why would anyone think that?" I said sarcastically.

"Yes, it was for good reason," he conceded. "Yet Professor Brain-Drain, who was there to serve a mere seven-day sentence, insisted on being placed in my cell. Rather than irritate a villain who could drain away his intelligence, the warden gave in and I got my first cell mate in forty years."

"Why would the Professor have done that?" I asked.

"Ego, of course," the Red Menace replied. "Even

after forty years behind bars, I still had the reputation as the worst villain in Superopolis's history, at least among those who still remembered me. It seemed that the Professor took issue with that, feeling he deserved the honor. We argued the entire seven days over which of us was the worst threat the city ever faced."

"That's an honor to aspire to," I said with disgust. "So who won?"

"Why I did, of course," he said and smirked. "When he was discharged seven days later, Professor Brain-Drain left without his power—while I retained every bit of my intelligence."

"But how?" I asked, fascinated to hear the answer.

"It was an accident, actually," he admitted. "On the

day he arrived, he taunted me by claiming my power was useless against him. He insisted he was far too intelligent to be manipulated. He was probably right. Yet when our first meal together arrived, I casually mentioned to him that he hated potato chips, and that they would dull his intelligence."

"He made exactly that comment the first time we met," I said as Professor Brain-Drain's puzzling statement finally made sense to me.

"It was brilliant. He wasn't expecting such a low-key command from me and it slipped through and settled in his brain," the Red Menace said, sneering. "I had manipulated him without his even knowing it. Of course, I had no idea what the result of this would be. I had merely done it in order to get his share of chips at every meal along with my own."

"And without the chips, Professor Brain-Drain's power vanished," I said.

"Exactly. We fought bitterly all week over who was the most evil, and by the end of his seven-day term, he was so angry that he decided to drain my intelligence and leave me behind in prison with my head an empty shell."

"Only he couldn't," I stated.

"No, he couldn't." The Red Menace smirked. "Of course I let him think he had, but it was clear to me that his power had failed. It didn't take me long to figure out why. I had always suspected that potatoes had unique properties. In fact, I had been experimenting with them myself during my original scheme."

"Yes, my friends and I were strapped onto your potato smasher several weeks ago by the Multiplier," I admitted.

"I had created that device to extract liquid from potatoes to use as a way of gaining power over the population," he explained. "But it wasn't until my innocent command to Professor Brain-Drain that I figured out the true power of the potato. And now you, too, have figured out the secret. It only confirms something I've been suspecting for several days—ever since you came to the hospital to see the Amazing Indestructo."

"What's that?" I asked, not sure I wanted to know the answer.

"That I need to get his Pseudo-Chip business under my complete control," he replied. "The Amazing Indestructo is a weak fool, and I saw from your visit how easily he might be persuaded to sell his business. So I've decided he *is* going to sell it—to me!"

"Why would he do that? Have *you* come up with a billion dollars?"

"One doesn't need a billion dollars if one has the ability to *order* someone to sell," he explained. "So far,

I've had no need to use my power on the simpleminded, selfish buffoon. But that doesn't mean I can't. The Pseudo-Chip business will be safely in my hands by tomorrow morning."

"And all for the sake of power," I concluded.

"Knowledge is the real power," the elderly villain said calmly as he began to shuffle toward me. "And the effect of Dr. Telomere's chips is the most important piece of knowledge ever. No one else can know it but me. So I'm afraid I have no choice but to eliminate you."

CHAPTER THIRTY-FOUR

The Fall of Captain Radio

Just as the Red Menace was about to lunge at me, an enormous roar pierced the silence of city hall. The villain froze in his tracks, and a look of sheer terror spread across his face. Clutching at his chest, he staggered back toward his son's desk.

I spun around and found myself face-to-face with Gore, the velociraptor. No wonder city hall was deserted.

There was a man-eating dinosaur roaming through it. Correction, a *meat*-eating dinosaur. I hoped he was still holding to his principles.

"You look like you could use some assistance," he said dryly. "I suggest we get you out of here."

I wasn't going to argue. I took off running while Gore trailed behind, making sure the Red Menace wasn't following. It wasn't until we were clear of city hall and approaching the northeast corner of Lava Park that I came to a stop.

"Thank you," I said as Gore stopped alongside me. "You saved my life."

"Think nothing of it." He waved a razor-sharp claw dismissively. "I guess that makes us even."

"What were you doing in city hall?"

"I had merely come to propose a solution to the mayor regarding the current conflict between animals and humans." He shrugged. "But he—and everyone else—fled screaming from the building before I could get two words out. I was searching the entire complex for someone and had just returned to the mayor's office when I witnessed your exchange with that menacing fellow."

"Did you hear what we were discussing?" I asked.

"Indeed I did," Gore admitted. "And now I under-stand why the powers of some of my animal friends have begun to fade. With the exception of a few bags that I still retain, the zoo ran out of chips the same night you paid us a visit. That was the main reason I came to bargain with the mayor."

"I don't understand." I shook my head.

"I had hoped to negotiate for better care for the animals of Superopolis while we still had leverage," he explained. "With our powers fading, I knew this might be the only opportunity."

"But now you know how to keep your powers going," I said, not sure this was a good thing.

"I honestly don't think that would be beneficial," Gore said to my complete surprise. "The animals have used their powers even more frivolously than you humans. For example, the monkeys still throw their own poop at each other, only now they do it from midair. Even worse, the carnivores among us have been using their powers to prey on the weaker species, and nothing I say will stop them. That's the primary reason things need to return to the way they were."

"I doubt humans would ever willingly give back powers they had been granted," I proposed.

"Neither would these animals," Gore countered. "That's why I'm making the decision for them. Not unlike the way, I am guessing, you have made the decision for the members of your own species."

Gore could tell from the look on my face that he had guessed right.

"You've made the right decision," he replied. "Despite your species' obvious flaws, you often use the powers bestowed on you to work together for the greater good and for the protection of the least among you. It's a noble endeavor and I compliment you on it."

I didn't know what to say.

"So get on with your plan," Gore concluded, "and I'll prepare my fellow creatures for the change that is imminent for them."

With that, he plunged into a woody area of Lava Park, leaving me bewildered yet oddly proud. But there was no time to waste. I still had no way to get the word out about switching back to Dr. Telomere's chips, and now I had to prevent the Red Menace from taking over the Amazing Indestructo's Pseudo-Chip business, too. I was going to need help.

I hurried as fast as I could to Needlepoint Hill. There were only two heroes I could turn to for help in dealing with the Red Menace—the same two heroes who had helped defeat him once before. The elevator car was waiting for me at the base of the mountain, and I let it carry me to the main level of Pinprick Manor. Once again, Lord Pincushion was awaiting my arrival, only this time he looked distinctly different. There wasn't a single sharp object sticking out of him anywhere.

"What happened to your . . ." I started to say.

"My accoutrements?" he finished my sentence, but not with the word I was searching for. "I deemed it prudent to remove them—at least until the mystery of these vanishing powers is solved. To lose my power while fully armed could be lethal."

Of course he had no way of knowing that Pinprick Manor's supply of Dr. Telomere's chips would keep their powers maintained. That was a secret I needed to keep.

"But regardless, welcome," he continued. "To what do we owe the pleasure of this visit?"

"It's the Red Menace," I said. "He's behind the vanishing powers, and I don't know what to do. That's why I've come to see you."

"I suspected his involvement," Lord Pincushion said with concern. "Come, let's find the Animator. It's just about time for our evening cocktails, so I expect we'll encounter him in the conservatory."

Striding briskly through the marvelous house, Lord Pincushion led me to a room that was small but well decorated with expensive-looking furniture. As he had predicted, there we found the Animator. He was bent slightly, examining some roses in a vase. They were bright red and vibrant looking.

"That really isn't a solution," Lord Pincushion said as we entered. "They're still dead, and your animating them won't change that fact."

"Well, at least they'll look good while we're sitting here. I'll pick new ones tomorrow," he added as he turned around and spotted me.

"Ordinary Boy!" he said and his face lit up. As he turned his attention to me, the roses instantly turned drab and wilted.

"I didn't think your power worked on living things,"

I said with amazement.

"Oh, it doesn't." He shook his head. "But when they're dead, it's a different story. The only problem is that it takes my full attention."

He turned back to the flowers and they revived again, looking fresh and alive.

"I guess I'm just lucky to still have my power." He shrugged.

"That's why the boy has come," Lord Pincushion explained as he motioned me toward one of the chairs. He and the Animator sat as well. "It appears that the Red Menace has shown his hand, and is in fact the person responsible for this astounding occurrence."

"It's true." I nodded. "And I need to know how you defeated him the last time."

"Ah, yes, that's quite a story," Lord Pincushion reminisced, "but in truth a very simple one."

"It was thanks to MagnoBox," the Animator explained. "We utilized his power to overcome the Red Menace."

MagnoBox was another of the original members of the League of Goodness, along with the Bee Lady, my two hosts, and Zephyr, who died several years ago. MagnoBox could broadcast real-time events on the TV that sat atop his shoulders.

"We took a page right out of the Red Menace's playbook," Lord Pincushion explained. "In the same way that he had used Captain Radio to spread his message to all Superopolis, MagnoBox did him one better. Television was a new technology in those days, and not one the Red Menace fully understood."

"It proved his downfall," the Animator commented.

"Indeed," agreed Pincushion. "We let the Menace capture us, and in the process he fell right into our trap. Not understanding MagnoBox's power, he told us everything he truly thought about the people of Superopolis and explained exactly how he planned to manipulate them. MagnoBox broadcast the whole thing, and the whole city finally saw the truth."

"That broke his spell and the Red Menace was finished," the Animator concluded.

"I don't suppose it would work again?" I asked. It was a long shot, but I needed some way to get my message out now that the mayor wasn't an option.

"Unlikely." Lord Pincushion shook his head. "MagnoBox is too old and has most likely lost his power as well. And the Red Menace would never fall for the same trick again anyway."

"I wasn't thinking of MagnoBox," I said as I pulled out my copy of the *Li'l Hero's Handbook*. "I was thinking of Captain Radio."

I flipped to his entry, but then quickly realized how impossible that idea would be.

NAME: Captain Radio. **POWER:** Possessing all the powers of radio waves, the Captain could broadcast over them, pick up their transmissions, and travel instantaneously by way of them. **LIMITATIONS:** A failure to understand the full reach of his abilities. **CAREER:** The greatest hero of his generation, his reputation was destroyed when he became the unwitting accomplice of the Red Menace. **CLASSIFICATION:** Riding the airwaves from supreme arrogance to utter humiliation left Captain Radio a broken man till the day he died.

"I'm afraid he's been dead for decades," the Animator explained. "He never did recover from the humiliation of having aided the Red Menace. He lived for quite some time after that event, but his career and reputation were destroyed. He died a very bitter man."

"Of course, that doesn't mean he can't still help us," Lord Pincushion said to my complete shock as he rose from his seat. "I think it's time we paid him a visit."

CHAPTER THIRTY-FIVE

Cold Storage

The sun had set and the moon was sitting high in the sky as I followed close behind the Animator and Lord Pincushion. They both moved slowly as we made our way to the industrial park in the southern part of town.

What they had in mind was a complete mystery to me. One minute they were talking about how Captain Radio was dead, and the next they were discussing what he may be able to do to bring down the Red Menace. Had senility caught up with the two elderly heroes? That suspicion grew stronger as we came to a halt in front of the Corpsicle Coolant Corporation.

"My mom works here!" I exclaimed.

"Does she?" the Animator asked in surprise. "Do you know what she does?"

"She freezes things." I shrugged. "That's her power."

The two heroes exchanged a knowing glance before turning and heading up the main sidewalk toward the entrance. When we got to the front door, it was obvious the building was closed for the evening. That didn't stop Lord Pincushion though, who rolled up his sleeve to reveal that he still had one sharp item stuck in his forearm—a thin, delicate pick.

"This should do the trick," he said. With lightning-like speed he inserted the pick in the lock of the door and in only a second had it opened. "Quick, let's get inside."

The three of us entered and found ourselves in a dark lobby. I had never actually been inside the place where my mother worked. I looked around, but it was difficult to make out my surroundings in the dimly lit space. As best I could tell, it looked about as warm and inviting as a dentist's office. My two coconspirators quickly headed for another door and I hurried to stay with them.

"The Corpsicle Coolant Corporation is involved in a number of businesses. I fear it may be a bit of a surprise to you as to what one of them actually is," Lord Pincushion explained as we made our way down a long, sterile-looking corridor and stopped in front of a large, thick door. "But it really isn't so strange if you think about it."

I had no idea what he was talking about, and my curiosity only grew as he pulled open the door and a blast of chilled air hit us head-on. Without additional comment, Lord Pincushion entered the room, and I followed him. The Animator brought up the rear. We were now standing in another long corridor, this one lined with glass doors, not unlike the frozen foods section of the Mighty Mart.

As I looked through the first of the glass doors, I realized this was no grocery store. The case held the body of a man—and he was completely frozen. What's more, I recognized him. It was Zephyr. Only he had died fifteen years ago.

"W-what's going on here?" I asked in alarm. "Is that really Zephyr?"

"It is." Lord Pincushion nodded somberly. "Shortly before he died, he made the decision to be frozen. As did all these other heroes and even a few villains."

He waved his arm down the extensive row of glass coolers, and my jaw dropped.

"But why?" was all I was able to say. "And how?"

"For an opportunity to live again, of course," the Animator explained.

"At some point a hero will come along who has

the ability to cure the incurable," Lord Pincushion explained. "Or, more amazingly, restore life."

"The Zombie Master was able to do that—sort of," the Animator interjected.

"Well, yes, but that was a rather unfortunate incident," Lord Pincushion said, dismissing the comment. "We're talking true life. And that's what these individuals are all patiently awaiting."

He hadn't answered the "how" part of my question, but he didn't need to. I couldn't believe my mother did something so *cool* and had never told me about it! The two older heroes led me down the central corridor of the chamber. As I rubbed my bare arms in an attempt to stay warm, I glanced at the frozen figures. I didn't recognize any of them after Zephyr—until we reached a specific case and my tour guides came to a halt. The hero behind the glass may have been frozen solid, but I recognized him immediately. It was Captain Radio.

For a moment, I wondered again why we were here. And then I remembered the Animator's power and what he had done with that vase of wilted roses. An instant later, the frozen corpse of Captain Radio slowly began to open its eyes.

CHAPTER THIRTY-SIX

Dead Giveaway

There was a light morning fog all around me as I stood below Stench's window and tossed pebbles at it. It only took three before his head appeared at the window. From the way he was rubbing his eyes, I could tell that I had woken him up.

"What's going on?" he said, partly curious and partly annoyed. "You know it's seven A.M., don't you?"

I knew. My parents had been up even earlier. They, the rest of the New New Crusaders, and now the laid-off members of the League of Ultimate Goodness were getting an early start at Dr. Telomere's Potato Chip Factory.

"It's an emergency," I said, whispering as loudly as I could. "Get dressed and meet me at headquarters."

Ten minutes later as I sat in our tree house base of operations, Stench's head popped through the entrance in the floor, his hair still a rumpled mess.

"This better be good," he said as he stifled a yawn.

"It's incredibly important," I explained. "I've found out that the Red Menace is definitely behind everybody's stolen powers, and we're the only ones who can stop him."

"It's AI's chips." Stench smacked a fist into his hand. "I knew it."

"Right," I said. That was the story I needed everybody to believe. "And this morning he's planning on getting AI to sign the chip business over to him altogether. Once that happens, it might be impossible to stop him."

"Can't we just tell everybody the chips are taking away their powers?" he asked.

"You saw how difficult it's been to get people to stop eating them even when we tell them face-to-face," I said. "I even tried to find Mayor Whitewash, so he could convince everyone, but the Red Menace still has him under his power."

"I see the problem," Stench said, deep in thought, as he turned for the first time toward the club's couch. It was only then that he noticed the figure seated there covered with a sheet.

"What the heck is this?!" he said in alarm.

"This is how we're going to destroy the Pseudo-Chip business once and for all," I grinned. I probably should have explained in more detail, but before I could Stench lifted up a corner of the sheet.

"Aaahhh!" he practically screamed as he leaped away from the couch. "There's a dead guy under here!"

The noise he made had to be audible for at least four square blocks. I probably would have laughed if I hadn't been concerned about attracting unwanted attention.

"Well, yeah," I admitted, "I guess you could look at it that way."

"Who is he?" he asked as he stayed safely away from the couch.

"This is Captain Radio," I explained as I removed the sheet entirely. The corpse had thawed and was creating a puddle on the floor and a big wet spot on the couch. "He's the last person the Red Menace will expect."

"Obviously," Stench said, still horrified. "He's dead! Have you gone insane? And what is he even doing here?"

"He walked here last night," I replied, knowing that I sounded completely nuts. "The Animator revived him. He was frozen, though, so he wasn't moving very fast. By the time we got to our neighborhood, we decided it was best to stash him here for the night and let him thaw out. Despite the difficulty of getting him up here."

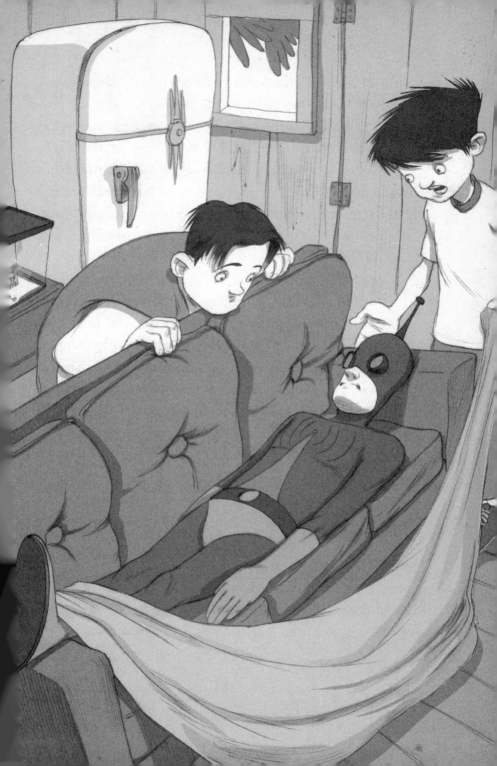

"Oh, well I guess *that* makes sense," Stench responded in a tone so sarcastic that even the corpse couldn't have missed it. "I see where he'd be a real threat to the Red Menace."

"Who's a threat?" a familiar voice asked as an *un*familiar head popped through the floor of the tree house. "No one's a bigger threat to you punks than me. And it's payback time for all the noise you've been making this morning."

While he definitely sounded like Fuzz Boy, he just didn't look like him. The hair on the top of his head had been buzzed to practically nothing. And his usual attempt at sporting a goatee or a mustache or some sort of facial hair had become impossible with the loss of his power. His mom had used the opportunity to haul him in for a haircut. Turning to Stench, as he entered the club, he had his back to the inanimate guest on our couch.

"Even though he's younger," he started to say, "my brother has always been strong enough to defend himself from me. But not anymore."

With that Fuzz Boy attacked Stench, his fists raised. I don't know which of the two was more surprised as Stench effortlessly lifted Fuzz Boy into the air, and with barely a grunt, threw him across the clubhouse and onto the couch.

NAME: Fuzz Boy. **POWER:** The ability to grow hair on anything he touches. **LIMITATIONS:** The effects only last a couple of hours. **CAREER:** Makes good money growing beards on his friends to get them into movies they're too young to see. **CLASSIFICATION:** When a situation gets hairy, it's a good bet he's around.

"Stench! Your power is back!" I said, a big grin spreading across my face.

"It's about time," he said with a bluster that only slightly hid the enormous sense of relief in his voice. "I stopped eating those chips four days ago."

Of course I knew the real reason behind the return of his power was the Dr. Telomere's chips I had given him two days ago, but that thought was interrupted by a horrible scream.

"There's a dead guy here!" Fuzz Boy shrieked, as Stench and I both turned to find he had landed right in the lap of Captain Radio.

Just as Fuzz Boy tried scrambling to get away, Captain Radio's eyes suddenly shot open, and his ice-cold hands closed around Fuzz Boy's wrists. I had never in my life heard a more bloodcurdling scream.

"AIYYIIEE!!!" Fuzz Boy's wail pierced the morning fog. "Get him off me!"

He struggled frantically against the reanimated corpse until his hand broke free of Captain Radio's grip.

"W-who is this clean-cut young man, and why is he so frightened of me?" the captain asked in a shaky and confused voice. "Am I still a pariah?"

Before I had a chance to answer Captain Radio's question, Fuzz Boy made a frantic dash for the exit and let out another scream as he missed a rung on the ladder and fell to the ground. As I looked down after him, it came as no surprise that there were two other figures standing there.

"Based on this lad's reaction, I assume that our guest is still up there," Lord Pincushion commented dryly as he watched the fleeing figure of Fuzz Boy. "The Animator probably shouldn't have activated his power until we had assessed the situation."

"Never mind about him," I called down to the two legendary heroes. "We've got all Superopolis to save."

CHAPTER THIRTY-SEVEN

A Radio Revival

It took us forever to reach the hospital. Not to be critical of the walking dead, but "stumbling dead" would have been a more accurate description for Captain Radio's degree of mobility.

It wasn't completely his fault, though. The Animator was expending a huge amount of energy to keep the captain animated. But he was no youngster himself and he regularly lost control. Whenever it happened, Captain Radio reverted to a corpse and fell flat on his face.

"Oh, dear," fretted the Animator during the most recent occurrence. "I never expected this to be so draining."

He immediately reasserted his power, and Captain Radio lifted his head from where it had plopped into a curbside bed of geraniums.

"So tell me again," he said, continuing the same conversation he had been engaged in when he had lost power, "have folks finally tired of the fad of television and returned to the wonders of the radio?"

I glanced up at Lord Pincushion, who, to my relief, decided to field this one.

"Indeed," he fibbed, but then added a hint of truth.

"Superopolis actually has more radio stations than it did in your glory days."

"I am picking them up," Captain Radio announced, "but all I can get from them is the most horrific sort of cacophony and announcers offering to give away tickets to hear more of it. It's truly baffling."

"So your power is working?" I asked eagerly.

"Yes, my reception is fine," he said. "I haven't yet tried my broadcasting ability."

"How does that work exactly?" I asked.

"It's simple," he said. "I can take anything audible and send it through the air so that anyone can hear it anywhere in the city."

"Even if they don't have a radio?" Stench asked.

"Yes." The captain nodded somberly. "That was how the Red Menace used me to force his message onto the entire population of Superopolis. Prior to that experience, I had directed my broadcasts solely to people's radios where they could listen to them only if they wished to."

"But there's even more to your power, isn't there?" I prompted him.

"Oh, yes," Captain Radio answered wistfully. "There's my power to ride the radio waves."

"Well, that might move us along faster," Stench suggested. "Should we let him try?"

"Please do!" urged an exhausted Animator.

"Our destination is Crania-Superiore Hospital," Lord Pincushion informed him. "Do you know where it is, and do you think you can transport us all there?"

"Of course I know it," Captain Radio replied indignantly. "I died there!"

I wasn't even aware anything had happened when a moment later we were all standing in front of the hospital. Captain Radio indeed possessed an amazing power. Now I hoped that the final aspect of his ability was also fully functioning. My worries weren't alleviated as the captain took another tumble when the Animator lost control of him.

"Here," I said as I pointed to a hospital gurney sitting outside the front entrance. "Let's get him up on that."

Thanks to the return of Stench's power, it was no problem for him to lift the deadweight hero. I removed a folded sheet that had been lying on top of the cart while Stench laid him on the gurney.

"Do you understand what you need to do?" I asked Captain Radio after the Animator revived him once again.

"Of course," he said. "Today I can finally extract my revenge on the man who destroyed my career and redeem myself in the eyes of all Superopolis. It will be a chance for me to finally . . . rest . . . in . . . peace."

I couldn't help but feel sorry for the dead hero. He had been arrogant in his glory days by all accounts, but he had clearly paid for it a thousand times over.

"Then let's go do it," I said as I unfolded the clean white sheet and spread it over the supine Captain Radio. "No one will find anything odd about us moving around a dead body in a hospital."

Stench grabbed hold of the gurney from the back and began pushing it toward the entrance. Once through the main doors he went straight for the head nurse's station as the Animator, Lord Pincushion, and I followed. But there was no one to challenge us. Nurse Slaphappy was not at her normal post. I directed Stench toward the corridor on the right and guided him to the room where the Amazing Indestructo was recuperating. Stench rammed the gurney into AI's closed door and sent it crashing inward.

As we filed into the room behind the covered corpse we found the Red Menace holding out a paper for the Amazing Indestructo to sign while Nurse Slaphappy and the Tycoon looked on.

"Don't do it, AI!" I shouted as they all looked at us in surprise. "Don't sell him your potato chip business!"

"But maybe you were right," he said in a pitiful whine. "Maybe my chips *are* sapping everybody's powers. I'm already hearing that a few people are even starting to blame me."

"So take the chips off the market, you buffoon," snapped Lord Pincushion. "Don't just sell the problem to someone else."

"That would be a financial disaster," the Tycoon butted in. "If AI's going to give up a cash cow like the Pseudo-Chips, we—I mean he—needs to be well paid for it."

I, of course, knew that the Red Menace had no intention of paying anything for the business. He was using his power to convince the Amazing Indestructo

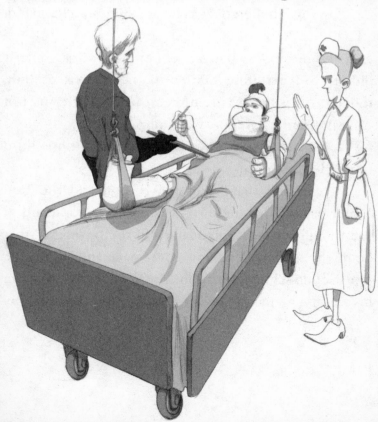

and the Tycoon to sign control over to him. Once they had, they'd never see a dime.

"If I don't make money, you don't make money," the Amazing Indestructo said to Lord Pincushion hoping for some support.

"Nobody needs money *that* badly," he snorted dismissively. "Have you really sunk to these depths?"

AI started to sob. "You're right. I'm despicable. Maybe I *should* just shut the business down."

"Nurse?" the Tycoon hollered in alarm. Nurse Slaphappy approached the pathetic figure of the Amazing Indestructo and gave him a smack across the face.

"Owww!" hollered AI as he recoiled from her hand. "That hurts!"

Like most everybody else, her power was gone. It didn't stop her from taking another whack at him, though. All it did was reinforce the inferiority part of AI's superiority-inferiority complex.

"Go ahead," he howled as she slapped him a third time. "I deserve it."

I could tell that both the Tycoon and the Red Menace, each for his own reason, were panicked at the thought that AI might not sell the business—that he might actually develop a conscience and shut down the Pseudo-Chips operation. But I never lost faith in his ability to make the wrong decision. In fact, my whole plan depended on it.

"Don't be distracted by Lord Pincushion or this boy," the Red Menace finally spoke, his voice carrying that compelling power even I could feel affecting me. "If it's true these chips are somehow sapping everybody's power, it could ruin you. Better to let me take on that potential problem."

"You're right," AI responded with hypnotic calm as he successfully blocked another oncoming smack from Nurse Slaphappy. "Everything will be better if I just unload this chip business. No one can blame me then!"

I honestly wonder how much this decision was a result of the Red Menace's power and how much was just the typical behavior of the Amazing Indestructo. Without even a twinge of guilt he signed the document the Red Menace held before him. I turned to the Animator, who had been standing silently in the corner, conserving his power, and gave him a silent nod. At the same moment, the Red Menace gripped the signed contract in his fist and raised it high in the air.

"Now no one can stop me!" he erupted in maniacal glee. "No one can take these chips off the market. And everyone will continue to buy them because I tell them to. The people of Superopolis are fools, and I, the

Red Menace, have the power to convince them that these tasteless, mealy mouthfuls of mush are actually something that they *like* to eat!"

The Red Menace howled. "Thanks to these chips, I have fulfilled my lifelong ambition to make everybody in Superopolis equal—everyone that is except *me*. And the simpering, simpleminded sheep of Superopolis will turn to *me* for guidance, never suspecting that it's their addiction to Pseudo-Chips that has robbed them of their powers."

"My chips *are* responsible?" AI cried out in alarm. "If only I'd known for sure!"

We all turned to look at him in disgust as Nurse Slaphappy again whacked his famous profile.

"You *will* take my name off the package, won't you?" the Amazing Indestructo asked meekly.

"Everyone knows that you're still the person who brought us these chips," I scolded AI.

The Red Menace looked at me suspiciously. He knew as well as I did that it wasn't the Pseudo-Chips that caused the problem. But the fact that I was pretending they were made him wary.

"Unfortunately, I'm going to need to eliminate anyone who knows the truth about my plans," the Red Menace continued . . . menacingly. "Thankfully, you're all together in this one room."

"If you're going to eliminate everyone who knows

they should stop eating the Amazing Indestructo's Amazing Pseudo-Chips," I informed him, "there won't be anybody left for you to control."

As a look of concern crept across the Red Menace's face, we heard a familiar whistle from out on the street. Rushing to the hospital window we were just in time to see a Dr. Telomere's delivery truck stopping in front of the hospital. It was being driven by Whistlin' Dixie.

"Y'all jes heard the Red Menace," she shouted through a bullhorn to a quickly gathering crowd. "He thinks yer jes dumb enough to keep eatin' the plum lousiest po-tato chips ever made—even if it costs y'all yer powers. Ah bet y'all are jes dyin' to go back to the best durn chips ever created."

With that, the back doors of the truck opened and there was Stench's dad, Windbag.

"I've stopped eating Pseudo-Chips," he informed the crowd, "and look at what I can do again."

With a huge gust of his breath he expelled the entire contents of the truck. Bags of Dr. Telomere's chips began to rain down on the eager and growing crowd. The Red Menace's mouth was agape as he watched the crowd grabbing for the bags of chips. His plan for total domination was at an end.

"How could this have happened?" the Red Menace said with barely controlled fury as he turned and glared directly at me. "How did everyone break free

of my power?"

"You convinced them yourself," I explained. "Everyone in Superopolis just heard everything you said. Even now the New New Crusaders and the League of Ultimate Goodness are fanning out around the city delivering the first new batches of Dr. Telomere's potato chips in weeks. No one will touch another Pseudo-Chip ever again."

"Whew! Thank goodness I sold the business," AI said, and then cringed in anticipation of a slap that never came. Everyone was too focused on the mounting rage of the Red Menace.

"But how?" he thundered. "No one has the power—"

"Don't they?" shouted the shrouded figure on the gurney, its sheet falling aside to reveal Captain Radio. "I still have the power!"

"I-i-impossible," shrieked the Red Menace. "You're dead!"

"And *you* killed me!" seethed the corpse of Captain Radio as he stood up from the gurney and began staggering toward the horrified villain. "*You* destroyed my reputation. *You* used my power to corrupt an entire city."

Real terror spread across the Red Menace's face,

making him look like the very old man he was. He tried backing away, but Captain Radio shuffled forward, raising his arms, his hands clutching as if he were going to strangle the person who had ruined his life.

"And now that very same power has destroyed *you*!"

Just as the living corpse lunged forward, the Animator lost, or purposely cut off, control. Captain Radio crumpled in a heap.

The Red Menace let out a gasping breath of relief. His reprieve was only short-lived, though, as he suddenly clutched at his chest, made an incomprehensible gurgling noise, and collapsed onto the floor alongside the hero who had—at last—redeemed himself.

CHAPTER THIRTY-EIGHT

The Hero Corpse

Over the next three days, people's abilities began to return. By Sunday, almost everyone had regained his or her power. Absolutely nobody realized it was because they had gone back to eating Dr. Telomere's chips. The blame for their power loss had been laid squarely at the feet of the Amazing Indestructo and his no-longer-so-amazing Pseudo-Chips. AI was already trying to salvage his reputation, but no one—not even the former LUGs—was buying it. He had finally managed to overestimate the gullibility and tolerance of the people of Superopolis.

For now the city had a new hero—Captain Radio!—at least until he was put back into cryogenic storage. A parade was held in his honor, and nearly everyone came out to see the procession as it traveled down the entire length of Colossal Way from Telomere Park all the way to downtown and Lava Park. Most of the time he remained an unresponsive corpse, but the Animator and Lord Pincushion were riding with him, and once every block the Animator revived him long enough for him to wave haphazardly and bask in the gratitude of the crowds. Even when he wasn't animated, he looked like the proudest corpse I'd ever seen.

I turned to my mom and dad, who stood with me on the sidewalk in front of the Superopolis Museum across from Lava Park, where we were watching the parade. My dad's hot hand was resting on one of my shoulders, and my mom's cool hand sat on the other. It was a pretty nice feeling. As the vehicle holding

Captain Radio approached, the captain waved directly at me for a moment, and then slumped back in his seat as he reverted to a corpse.

"Frozen vegetables?" I said skeptically to my mother.

"We do *mostly* produce frozen vegetables," she protested. "The dead people are only a sideline."

"Well, in addition to refreezing Captain Radio, you're going to have one more to take care of tomorrow," I said. "The Red Menace is going to be put on ice for real this time."

"All I can say is we should be grateful I have a job," she harrumphed. "Your father's team lost their first sponsor after only a week."

We both looked at my dad, who had a remarkably cheerful expression on his face for someone who was no longer getting paid to promote Maximizer Brand Snack Cakes. As he broke into a grin, it was clear he was trying to keep something secret.

"Okay, Thermo," my mom said with irritation. "What aren't you telling us?"

"Well . . ." he started to say, as he showed why he could never be trusted with a secret, "it won't be announced until tomorrow, so you have to promise to keep it to yourselves."

"We promise," we replied robotically.

"Tomorrow," he began eagerly, "the board of Dr.

Telomere's is going to announce that for the first time in its history it's hired a team to represent the chips."

"You're kidding!" I said in amazement. "That's—that's—humongous!!"

"Thermo, are you telling us . . ." my mom said, almost speechless.

"That's right." He beamed. "As of tomorrow, the New New Crusaders will be the exclusive spokesteam for the most popular—once again!—product in all Superopolis."

Just then, my fellow Junior Leaguers burst through the crowd and gathered around us. They couldn't help but notice the stunned look on my face.

"What's going on?" Stench asked suspiciously. "You and your dad have the same dopey expression that my dad was wandering around with all morning."

"Oh, nothing," I said trying to act nonchalant. "It's nothing at all."

"Well, come on, then," Tadpole said with irritation. "Let's head over to the park."

I waved good-bye to my parents just as they gave each other an enormous hug, and followed my teammates across the street to Lava Park. The Inkblot's newsstand was right in front of us, and the Inkblot was standing there talking the ear off an old lady who was only trying to buy a roll of breath mints.

"Why I was practically Captain Radio's sidekick,"

NAME: Inkblot, The. **POWER:** The ability to repel ink from his body. **LIMITATIONS:** Only able to write in pencil. **CAREER:** Owner and operator of Inkblot's Newsstand on the southeast corner of Lava Park. **CLASSIFICATION:** Still awaiting his big break as a crime fighter despite smudges on his record.

he was explaining as he stretched the truth like a piece of taffy. "I'm glad to see him looking so good. I thought I'd heard he had died, but you know the newspapers—they can't get anything right."

He was certainly right about that this time. I scanned the headlines. *The Hero Herald* said: POWERS RETURN AS PSEUDO-CHIPS BANNED! *The Superopolis Times* reported: POWER-SAPPING SECRET DIES WITH RED MENACE. Of course *The Daily Weekly* announced: PANIC SPREADS AS POWERS FAIL. But what mattered was that *everyone* believed that the Pseudo-Chips had robbed them of their powers. No one even suspected that it was the lack of Dr. Telomere's chips that had been responsible, and I wasn't going to correct them.

With the Red Menace dead, only Dr. Telomere and I knew the truth. However, the second I had that thought, I could have sworn I saw a reptilian figure peeking out from a wooded section of Lava Park. Just as quickly, it disappeared. I was certain it had to be Gore, and I realized that someone else did know—just not someone human.

But I lost track of him amid the crowd of people who were thronging the park. After all, the final mayoral debate was about to occur, and everyone was fascinated to see it in light of all the recent events.

The parade had been Mayor Whitewash's idea, and

that, along with the return of his power, had caused a significant uptick in his polls. It also hadn't hurt that the powers of the zoo animals had also vanished, and most of them were now safely back in their cages. The mayor was not only now leading the carved pumpkin, but he was even gaining on Professor Brain-Drain. I never did get a chance to pass along the crucial piece of information I had for him, so my plan was to do it now. But just in case things turned ugly again, I had also brought along my bodyguards.

"Stay in the middle of the ring we're going to form around you," Stench instructed. "Now that we've all got our powers back, it should be a breeze to keep you safe if we need to."

"I think everything will be fine," I said, "but thanks, you guys, for making sure."

The candidates were already up on the stage as we approached, and Professor Brain-Drain was in the middle of a speech.

". . . and that is why, despite the return of your powers, the reelection of Mayor Whitewash will bring nothing but pestilence, famine, and disease—in addition to other liberal objectives. That is why you must cast your votes for me."

"Well now," said Mayor Whitewash, sounding like his old confident self. "Professor Brain-Drain may not have a criminal record—"

"Excuse me, Mr. Mayor," I shouted out from the crowd. "But that's not exactly true."

A murmur rose from the crowd as everyone turned to look at me. My friends were all on high alert, but I knew I wasn't in any danger. Instead, I pushed my way to the stage and stepped onto the platform.

"What is the meaning of this, son?" asked the mayor.

"What Professor Brain-Drain said about not having a record isn't true," I said. The Professor's eyebrows narrowed to a scowl as he glared at me from behind his thick, blank glasses. "Professor Brain-Drain is a convicted criminal. And I have the proof."

The crowd began chattering in surprise as I whipped out the document I had found buried away amid a sea of paperwork and records down at city hall. I handed it to the mayor who scanned it quickly.

"The boy is right," he said as he looked back at the crowd. "Professor Brain-Drain's candidacy is illegal. Ten years ago, he served one week in prison—for failing to properly register a blimp."

EPILOGUE

The Race Is Run . . . or Only Begun?

Cannonball's team trounced mine in the elections on Tuesday. Don't even ask me why I was surprised. Despite having delivered on my promise to return everyone's powers before the election, my classmates decided they had already gotten what they wanted from us. Cannonball, on the other hand, had brought a bag of candy bars and offered to hand them out to anyone who voted for his side. It was a landslide.

The Spore had cemented his uncontested run when he showed up the day before with a campaign poster. It had shown a blown-up image of a photo he had gotten with himself and Captain Radio on Sunday. The poster read: CAPTAIN RADIO ENDORSES THE SPORE:

"HE'LL BE THE LAST GUY TO LET YOU DOWN," SAYS THE CAPTAIN.

I suspect he'll get lots of work as Transparent Girl's financial dealings lead to ever more fish floating to the top of our aquarium tank. Of course, I could just be bitter.

But the truth was I had other things on my mind as I made my way toward downtown and police headquarters after school. I had been summoned there by Professor Brain-Drain himself. I didn't *have* to accept his invitation, but something told me I should.

As I walked up the sidewalk toward police headquarters, I had the sudden impression I was being watched. Among all the people coming and going, I caught sight of a familiar figure sitting on one of the benches that lined the main pathway. It was Dr. Telomere.

"Well done, boy," I thought I heard him say. "And, remember, time will always tell."

I was just about to approach him when a figure stepped between us.

"I owe you an enormous debt of gratitude, young man," Mayor Whitewash said as he stuck out his hand for me to shake. "I doubt I would have won the election without your detective work."

"I'm sorry about your father," I replied. "I feel

responsible for that, too."

"I lost my father fifty years ago." The mayor shook his head sadly. "He chose to pursue a plan of domination rather than raise my brothers and me. It took all my abilities in my first election to convince the people of Superopolis that I was not my father's son. Besides, he was always embarrassed by me because I only had a pale version of his power."

As the mayor patted me on the shoulder and continued on, I thought how lucky I was to have a father who was proud of me with or without a power. And Dr. Telomere hinted that I might just yet turn out to have one. I turned back to the bench he had been sitting on, but it was now empty. I shrugged and continued on my way."

Once inside, I was led down a long gloomy hallway by a police officer and brought before a solid glass wall. On the other side stood Professor Brain-Drain.

"Prison isn't so bad the second time around," he said as my escort left us alone. "And, thankfully, the sentence for lying on a candidate registration form is only two weeks. I'll be out before you know it."

"And then what?" I asked.

"Well, for one thing, there's still a mountain-size chunk of prodigium waiting for me beneath Crater Hill."

"You wouldn't try using it to send everyone back

in time again, would you?"

"Of course not," he sneered. "I would never repeat myself. I don't need to. There is no end to the mischief I could make with the amount of power stored in that rock."

"Yet you still have no power of your own."

"Yes, you're right." He smiled sinisterly. "Everyone's abilities returned except mine. Why would that be?"

"Because everyone stopped eating the Pseudo-Chips," I said as I felt my nerves begin to twitch with concern.

"But I never *started* eating them," he pointed out. "It was only in the last twenty-four hours that I began to realize that the problem wasn't with what people were eating. It was what they *weren't* eating that had made all the difference. The same thing that I also haven't eaten for ten years now."

The feeling in my gut turned to icy fear, and the Professor could see it reflected in my eyes. It was only then that I noticed the bowl of potato chips sitting on the table in Professor Brain-Drain's cell.

"I have to give you credit, boy," he said as he casually reached toward the bowl and took a single chip from it. "Your manipulation of events this past week has been nothing less than masterful."

He raised the chip to his mouth and then paused.

As his hand began to shake, a look of revulsion crept across his face.

"You've kept the truth a secret from everyone," he said. "Everyone . . . but me."

And then he popped the potato chip into his mouth and began to chew.